Nothing looked wrong . . .

First thing the next morning, Kelly hurried down to the pool. If there was something wrong with the diving board, it would have to be repaired before the pool opened, or the diving board would have to be off-limits for the day.

The air was still a bit chilly that early in the morning. Kelly stuck her toe in the water. It felt warm. She walked over to the diving board and inspected it. Nothing looked wrong. She climbed the metal steps and stepped up onto the board. The surface felt wet from the morning dew. Kelly walked out to the end. The board bent and creaked slightly. She bounced gently up on her toes and felt the spring of the board. It felt okay to her.

She bent her knees and bounced again, this time springing higher into the air. The board bent, but felt firm when she landed. On the next bounce she sprang even higher. As she came down, her feet hit the board again.

Crack! The board snapped like a twig.

Splash!

Kelly hit the water face first.

**Read these other thrillers
available from HarperPaperbacks**

NIGHTMARE INN

THE POOL

T. S. Rue

HarperPaperbacks
A Division of HarperCollins*Publishers*

HarperPaperbacks   *A Division of* HarperCollins*Publishers*
          10 East 53rd Street, New York, N.Y. 10022

Produced by Daniel Weiss Associates, Inc., 33 West 17th Street, New York, New York 10011.

First printing: July, 1993

Printed in the United States of America

HarperPaperbacks and colophon are trademarks of HarperCollins*Publishers*

10 9 8 7 6 5 4 3

THE POOL

Chapter 1

"Someone asked for the New Arcadia?"

The voice sounded distant and vague. Next came some heavy footsteps.

"Hey, wake up."

Kelly Schneider felt someone shaking her shoulder. She opened her eyes and realized she'd fallen asleep. The bus driver, a fat man with greasy black hair, was standing in the aisle, staring at her.

"You were going to the New Arcadia, right?" he asked.

Kelly nodded. She yawned and stretched and looked around. She was sitting in a seat on a dimly lit bus. The bus had been half full when it left the city. Now Kelly was surprised to see that she and the driver were the only ones left.

"Where'd everyone go?" Kelly asked, still drowsy.

"Where'd they go?" The bus driver grinned. "I

murdered 'em and dumped them in a ditch. . . . Where do you think they went?"

Kelly eyed the bus driver nervously. His jaw was covered with whiskers, and his uniform looked as though it hadn't been washed in weeks. He was just creepy enough for Kelly to wonder if he actually might have killed the other passengers.

"They all got off already," the bus driver said, turning and going back down the aisle. "It ain't often I get someone who goes this far to the middle of nowhere."

He went to the front of the bus, pushed open the door, and got out. Kelly tried to look out the window, but all she could see was darkness. She reached up to the overhead rack and got down her portable CD player, and then got off the bus.

It was a moonless night. The air was damp, and a light mist floated through the trees. Kelly looked around. Both sides of the road were lined with thick woods. There wasn't a building or an electric light in sight. Not even a sign that said "bus stop."

The driver had pulled open a baggage bay and taken out Kelly's suitcase. Kelly walked toward him.

"Where is everyone?" she asked.

"Everyone?" The bus driver looked at her. "Who's everyone?"

"Well, I mean a town or a store or at least a bus

stop," Kelly said. "How do you know this is the right place to leave me?"

"I go by the odometer," the driver replied as he slammed the baggage bay shut. "Forty-seven point six miles from the last stop, and boom, you're here."

He walked back to the door and climbed in. Kelly put down her CD player and ran after him. He was just pulling the door closed when she stuck her head in.

"You're not just going to leave me here, are you?" she asked.

"Hey, I'm a bus driver, not a baby-sitter," he replied. The doors closed with a hiss.

The next thing Kelly knew, the engine revved and the bus pulled away. She was left in a cloud of diesel exhaust.

Coughing and waving the smoke out of her face, she watched the bus grow small as it drove away. Soon it was just two small red lights, then nothing.

Suddenly she realized how quiet it was. She was standing on the side of the road, hundreds of miles away from home, in the middle of nowhere—all alone. A thick layer of clouds covered the sky, making it so dark that Kelly could just barely see the outline of her suitcase a few feet away.

Kelly felt a shiver of nervousness. Now what? The letter hiring her as head lifeguard at the New Arcadia Inn had simply instructed her to tell the bus driver to drop her off at the stop for the inn. Kelly had assumed that there would be someone there to meet her. Or if there wasn't, at least there'd be a phone she could call from.

But there was nothing . . . nothing except the road, the woods, and darkness. Kelly sat down on her suitcase. She felt her stomach grow tight and start to hurt. Some people bit their nails when they were nervous. Some fidgeted. Kelly's stomach always started to hurt when she was tense. And right now she was *very* tense.

Kelly didn't like being tense. She didn't like feeling that things were out of control. She prided herself on being able to stay calm in high-pressure situations. It was part of what made her a good lifeguard.

Don't let it get to you, she told herself. *You said in your letter that you were coming tonight. Someone will show up sooner or later.*

Reaching down to the ground, she picked up her CD player and turned it on. Music started to play. It was a good thing she'd remembered to put new batteries in.

The music was good company, and for a song or two Kelly felt proud that she'd thought of a way to soothe herself in a difficult situation. But as the third song began she could feel her stomach tighten again.

Why hadn't anyone come yet? What if they hadn't gotten her letter? What would she do if no

4

one came? Where would she spend the night?

The bus driver had said it was forty-something miles from the last stop. It would take forever to walk back.

Kelly hugged herself and shivered. She wasn't cold; she was scared.

Maybe she shouldn't have taken this job after all. It was true that it paid fifty dollars a week more than the other inns and resorts that had wanted her, and after all, one of her goals this summer was to make as much money as she could for college. But the weird thing was that she couldn't remember sending a résumé to any place called the New Arcadia.

Of course, she'd sent out more than fifty letters, and it was quite possible that one of those places had changed its name. Or maybe the owner of one place was a friend of the owner of the New Arcadia, and her letter had been passed along. The truth was that Kelly hadn't given it much thought before. But now she wondered if she should have.

She sat through two more songs in the dark. Not a single car had passed since the bus dropped her off. Kelly looked nervously behind her at the shadowy tree trunks on the edge of the woods.

Were there wild animals in the woods?

Would they be attracted to the sound of the music?

Calm down, she told herself. A car was bound to come for her.

Sooner or later.

Suddenly Kelly heard a twig snap. She twisted around and gasped.

A dark figure was standing behind her.

Chapter 2

Kelly jumped up and backed away. The dark figure was only a few feet from her. It was a guy. She must not have heard him because of the music.

"Who . . . who are you?" she managed to squeak.

"Who do you think I am?" the guy asked as he stepped toward her. He sounded as if he was in his twenties. He wasn't that tall, but even in the blackness Kelly could see that he was stocky and strongly built.

"This isn't funny," Kelly said. Her heart was beating hard and she was breathing too quickly. Her stomach was really cramping up. "If you don't tell me who you are, I'll scream."

"Do you really think anyone would hear you?" the guy asked.

He was right. Kelly started to look around for

something to fight him off with . . . or a place to run to.

"Hey, chill out," the guy said. "My name's Martin, and I'm from the inn."

Kelly felt somewhat relieved, but not entirely. "Where's your car? How'd you get here? Where's the inn?"

"Hey, one question at a time, okay?" Martin said as he picked up Kelly's suitcase.

"Where are you taking that?" Kelly asked.

"I figured I'd take it to the inn, unless there's someplace else you'd like to go," Martin replied. He started to walk across the road, then stopped and looked back. "You coming?"

Kelly picked up her CD player and followed. "You walked here?"

"Yeah. The inn's not real big on giving out cars." Martin crossed the road and headed into the trees. Kelly followed him to the edge of the woods, then stopped. Martin looked back at her. "Now what's wrong?"

"I'm sorry, Martin," Kelly said. "You came out of nowhere. I have no idea who you are. I feel a little funny following you into the woods in the middle of the night."

"Well, I was going to take a shortcut," Martin said. "It's about half a mile through the woods. If we stay on the road it's more like two miles."

Kelly thought it over. "I think I'd prefer the road."

Martin shrugged. "Suit yourself."

He stepped back up to the road and started walking along it. Kelly followed him again.

"Are you the one who hired me?" she asked.

"Nope."

"What do you do at the inn?"

"I'm in charge of teen recreation."

"Then you're my boss."

"Well, no. Running the pool is separate," Martin said.

"Is this your first year?"

"At the inn?" Martin asked. "Nope."

"Well, how long have you been working there?" Kelly pressed.

"I'll tell you, Kelly," he said. "It seems like I've been there forever."

"Forever, huh? What's it like?"

"It's an incredible place," Martin said. "Once you've been there awhile, you'll probably never want to leave."

The road sloped downhill, and as they walked along, the mist turned thicker. Now it was almost a heavy, damp fog. Kelly felt a chill. She was following some stranger named Martin through a foggy night down an empty road to a place she'd never been before.

After a while the inn came into view, and Kelly was finally able to relax a bit. The New Arcadia was a large, white, three-story colonial building, set in a clearing surrounded by woods. The grounds were well-lit, and Kelly could see that the inn appeared well taken care of. There were quite a few cars in the parking lot, which reassured Kelly further. Martin had told her a little more about the place as they'd walked, so she knew there was a spa in back with an indoor-outdoor pool and other facilities.

"Most of the staff stays on the third floor," Martin said as they went inside the main building. They crossed the lobby and passed a large stone fireplace. "I figured you might want a room overlooking the swimming pool, so you can keep an eye on things."

They entered a corridor, and Martin stopped in front of an elevator. He pushed the up button, and a second later the doors opened. Before Martin and Kelly could step in, two guys and a girl stepped out. One of the guys was short, with curly brown hair and bad skin. The other guy was taller and really cute. He had light-brown hair and green eyes. The girl was thin and athletic looking, with short blond hair.

"Hey, Martin!" the curly-haired guy said. "Everyone's going over to the disco. You want to come?"

"Maybe later, Eric," Martin said. "I want you guys to meet your new boss, Kelly Schneider."

"Whoa!" Eric stared at her. "*You're* the new head lifeguard?" He puffed out his chest and shook her hand. "Welcome to the New Arcadia, and may I personally be at your service should you need anything."

"I'm Tiffany," said the girl with the short blond hair. She seemed kind of cold.

Kelly turned to the handsome guy.

"This is Nick," Eric said. "He's not a lifeguard, but he hangs out with us."

"Nice to meet you," Nick said, shaking Kelly's hand and gazing into her eyes. He smiled, but seemed very reserved. Kelly might have stared up at him a second too long.

"I think we better get over to the disco," Tiffany said. She seemed eager to go.

"Hey, what's the rush?" Eric asked, turning again to Kelly. "Maybe you want to join us."

"Well, thanks, but I just got here," Kelly replied, although she glanced at Nick to see how he reacted to the idea.

"Come on, Eric," Tiffany said. "Can't you see she has to get unpacked and settle in? You'll see her tomorrow morning. Nine A.M. sharp, remember?"

"That's right," Martin said to Kelly. "I arranged for a meeting for you and the other lifeguards in the morning. So you could get to know each other."

"Well, I might stop by the disco later anyway," Kelly said. "How long do you think you'll be there?"

She aimed the question at Eric, but it was really Nick who she hoped would be there.

"As long as it takes," Eric said with a wink. "I'll wait all night for you."

Kelly smiled.

"You're probably tired after your trip," Tiffany said insistently. "I know you'll probably want to take it easy tonight. You shouldn't feel like you *have* to meet everyone this instant. We'll all be there in the morning."

"I know." Kelly nodded. Nick, Tiffany, and Eric said good-bye and headed across the lobby. Martin and Kelly got into the elevator.

"They're a good group," Martin said. "I'm sure you'll all get along fine."

"Have any of them worked here before?" Kelly asked.

"Uh, no."

"No one came back from last year?"

"The New Arcadia wasn't open last year," Martin said. "Actually, it's been closed since the early seventies. It just reopened a few months ago."

Kelly frowned. "I thought you said you've been here forever."

Martin shrugged. "Figure of speech."

The elevator doors opened again, and Martin stepped out into the third-floor corridor. Kelly followed him. Martin walked all the way down the hall to the very last room. He pushed open the door and went in.

"Oh, hello, Sebastian," she heard him say. Kelly stepped into the room. A man with gray hair pulled into a ponytail was standing inside the door. He was wearing paint-stained overalls and a work shirt. Silver-and-turquoise Indian jewelry adorned his fingers and wrists. Martin introduced them.

"Sebastian's in charge of the waterfront," Martin said. "He's also the inn's handyman. Sebastian, I want you to meet Kelly Schneider, our new head lifeguard."

"Delighted," Sebastian said.

"Is there something wrong with the room?" Martin asked, pointing at the toolbox on the floor.

"Not really," Sebastian said. "Just a little problem with the door lock." He turned to Kelly and held up a lock cylinder. "I've got to get a replacement for this. You won't mind staying here until I do, will you?"

"Why would I mind?" Kelly asked.

"Well, you won't be able to use your lock," Sebastian said.

"You mean, I won't be able to lock my door?" Kelly asked.

"It'll just be a day or two," Sebastian said.

"Is there another room I can stay in?" Kelly asked, turning to Martin.

"All the other staff rooms are being used," Martin said. "Tiffany and Claire share a room. I guess we could put a cot in there with them."

Kelly looked around. Based on the not-so-friendly reception she'd just gotten from Tiffany, she didn't think she wanted to share a room with her. Kelly's room was small and had a single bed. Against the opposite wall was a desk and chair. In her letter Kelly had mentioned that she would prefer to room alone.

"I really don't think you have to worry," Martin said with a smile. "It's pretty safe around here."

"But what about when I'm at the pool?" Kelly asked. "Someone could come in here without my knowing."

"Well, you could leave your valuables in the safe at the front desk," Martin suggested. "It'll only be for a day or so, right, Sebastian?"

"A day or so at the most," Sebastian replied with a nod.

"Well, okay, I guess." Kelly wasn't happy about it, but she didn't want to sleep on a cot in someone else's room, either.

"Welcome to the New Arcadia, Kelly," Sebastian said, picking up his toolbox. "I hope you like it here."

Sebastian left, and Martin put down her suitcase and went to the window.

"There she is," he said.

Kelly stepped to the window and looked out. Below her was the pool. It was shaped like an hourglass, with two wide ends joined by a narrow passage in the middle. One of the wide ends was indoors and enclosed under a steel and glass canopy. The other half was outdoors. Underwater lights shone beneath the surface, turning the water an aqua-blue color.

Martin went back to the door. "If you have any problems with anything, just give me a yell."

"Thanks," Kelly said.

Martin went out and pulled the door closed behind him. As soon as Kelly was alone, she took the chair from the desk and wedged it against the door so that no one could get in. Then she sat down on the bed and tried to relax. It was a strange beginning to her new summer job. Hopefully things would soon become more normal.

Chapter 3

After unpacking her things, Kelly went to the bathroom to take a long, hot shower. Thankfully the bathroom door locked, so she knew she'd have some privacy. After her shower she got out her hair dryer and blew her blond hair dry. Looking at herself in the mirror, she thought of Eric's reaction when he had first seen her. It was obvious that he had thought she was pretty. Kelly was used to guys telling her she was good-looking. Some guys had even said she was beautiful, but Kelly had never been certain whether they meant it or were just saying it because they wanted something. She had large blue eyes, high cheekbones, and clear, pale skin. Her nose was just ever so slightly bent. It had been that way since birth, and Kelly really didn't mind. She felt lucky to have the looks she had, and didn't feel any need to be perfect.

She found her makeup case and put on a little

makeup. She never wore a lot; sometimes she didn't wear any at all. But she already knew she was going to stop in at the disco tonight. Kelly had two goals for the summer. One was to make money. The other was to have fun—lots of fun.

After getting dressed in a T-shirt and jeans, she collected her jewelry and put it in a small zippered bag to take down to the front desk. There were a few pieces Kelly wanted to keep safe. One was a small gold cross on a gold chain that her grandmother had given her. Another was a silver ring with an opal. As she left the room, she paused and looked back. She was leaving her CD player, some CDs, and all her clothes. She hoped Martin was right when he said this place was safe.

At the front desk a young woman wearing a white blouse and a black bow tie smiled at Kelly. She had curly red hair and haunting eyes. A small name tag above her pocket said her name was Sarah.

"Uh, hi," Kelly said, placing her jewelry bag on the counter. "I'd like to leave some things in the safe."

Sarah frowned. "Are you staying here?"

"No, I'm the new head lifeguard. I work here."

"I'm sorry, but the safe is for guests only," Sarah said.

"Well, the problem is the lock on the door to my room is broken," Kelly explained. "Martin said

18

I could keep my jewelry in the safe until Sebastian fixed it."

"I'll have to talk to the manager," Sarah said. "Just wait here."

Kelly watched the red-haired girl go to the end of the counter and disappear through a door. She didn't understand why putting a few things in the safe was such a big deal. Kelly wondered if maybe Sarah was sick; she had dark circles under her eyes, and her skin was unnaturally pale.

A few moments later Sarah returned. "All right," she said. "He said we'll hold your jewelry for now. But as soon as your door's fixed you'll have to come get it."

"Uh, thanks," Kelly said. "And can you tell me how to get to the disco?"

"Down through those doors and past the dining room," Sarah said. Kelly noticed that Sarah's eyelids never blinked. She figured that the red-haired girl really wasn't feeling well.

Kelly soon found herself following the sound of loud music down the hall. The disco was in a room lined with floor-to-ceiling windows. Through the glass she could see people standing at the bar and others sitting in booths. The music blasted loudly and colored lights flashed and sparkled through the room. But no one was dancing.

Kelly suddenly felt shy. It wasn't like her to just join a group of strangers in a noisy disco. For a moment she stood outside, trying to decide what to do. Maybe she should go back to her room and wait to meet everyone in the morning. She turned and started to walk back down the corridor.

"Hey, Kelly!" a voice shouted.

Kelly turned. Eric was standing in the doorway of the disco.

"Where do you think you're going?" he asked.

Kelly felt a little embarrassed. She didn't want to admit that she'd been too shy to go in.

"Hey, come on," Eric said, walking toward her. "No one's going to bite you."

Kelly smiled. "I know."

Together they walked back into the disco. The music was unbelievably loud inside; the floor shook with the sound coming from the speakers. Eric led Kelly to a booth where Tiffany and Nick were sitting. A pitcher of soda sat on the table, next to some glasses. Tiffany gave Kelly a little smirk. She and Nick were sitting on the same side of the booth, and she slid a little closer to him when Kelly sat down opposite them. Nick gave Kelly a short, mysterious smile.

"It's a good thing I went out and got her," Eric said, sitting down next to Kelly. "She almost got away." He poured her a glass of soda. "So how'd you wind up getting a job at this place?"

Kelly told the others about how she'd sent letters to a whole bunch of resorts. "The funny thing is, I don't remember sending one to the New Arcadia."

"That's weird—the same thing happened to me!" Eric said. "I just figured they must have gotten my name from one of the other places I wrote to. What about you, Tiffany?"

It turned out Tiffany didn't remember sending an application to the New Arcadia either. Eric turned to Nick. "I know you're not working here, but how'd you know about this place?"

"I heard about it from someone," Nick replied.

"Another insightful answer from the mystery man," Eric said.

"You're here alone?" Kelly asked.

Nick nodded. It seemed a little odd to Kelly. She guessed that he was seventeen or eighteen. Why would someone his age come to a resort alone?

"Don't try figuring Nick out," Eric said. "He won't tell you anything about himself. My guess is that he's in the CIA. Either that or he's an alien who's come to study our culture."

Kelly looked at Nick, watching the shadows and light fall on his face. Even if he avoided talking about himself, there was something undeniably attractive about him.

A new song started playing.

"Oh, Nick!" Tiffany gasped, suddenly sliding her hand through his arm and pulling him out of the booth. "This is my favorite song. You have to dance with me."

Kelly watched as Tiffany dragged Nick out of the booth and onto the dance floor. It was obvious that Tiffany really liked him. The question was whether Nick felt the same way. The next thing Kelly knew, Eric turned to her with a big grin.

"Feel like dancing?" he asked.

Kelly did, but not with him. Still, she didn't want to be a drip, so she said yes and followed him onto the dance floor.

Kelly stayed at the disco much later than she'd planned. A couple of other lifeguards and their friends showed up. Kelly danced with Eric and then with a guy named Chip. With the exception of Tiffany, everyone was very friendly to her. Several times during the evening, Kelly glanced at Nick and found him gazing back at her. She wished she could have danced with him, but it seemed as though Tiffany stayed by his side every minute.

Finally Kelly knew she had to go to bed. She told everyone that she'd see them in the morning.

"How about one last dance?" Eric asked.

"I'm sorry, Eric, but we've got a full day of work tomorrow," she said as she got up. "I really have to get some sleep."

"Well, okay, it's pretty late," Eric said. "Maybe I better walk you back to your room."

A couple of people sitting around the table smiled at each other. Kelly knew they must be thinking that Eric had the hots for her. Kelly's eyes met Nick's one last time. He looked a little amused. If only *he'd* wanted to walk her back.

"It's okay," Kelly told Eric. "You really don't have to."

"But I *want* to," Eric insisted.

Not wanting to be mean, Kelly agreed. They took the elevator up to the third floor and walked along the quiet hallway.

"This summer was really starting to look like a bummer until you showed up," Eric said.

"What do you mean?" Kelly asked.

"Well, the only other girl lifeguards are Tiffany and Claire," Eric said. "And Tiffany has a massive crush on Nick. Claire, well, you haven't met Claire yet. She tends to stay in her room. She's not my type. I mean, she's nice and everything, but she's a little too quiet and scared of her own shadow."

"Maybe you should try to get to know her better," Kelly said, hoping Eric would get the subtle hint.

"I'd rather get to know you," Eric said.

"That's nice, Eric," Kelly said. She knew she was going to have to come up with some way to let him know she wasn't interested. They got to her door.

"So, uh, I had fun tonight," Eric said.

"Me, too."

"You're really a good dancer."

"You're not bad yourself," Kelly replied, trying

23

to hide her discomfort. Eric obviously didn't want to leave.

"So, uh, I guess I'll see you in the morning," Eric said with a nervous smile.

It was just the excuse Kelly needed. She looked down at her watch and pretended to gasp. "Oh, no! It already is the morning. I'd love to stand here and talk with you, Eric, but I really have to get some sleep."

The smile on Eric's face was replaced by a look of disappointment. "Oh, uh, yeah. So, I'll see you later." He started back down the hall. Kelly watched for a moment, then breathed a sigh of relief and pushed open her door.

She flicked on the light and suddenly froze.

Someone had been in her room!

Chapter 4

Kelly pressed her back against the door and stared around the room. Her heart started to race, and she felt her chest grow tight. She was certain she hadn't left her bathrobe lying over the back of the chair, or her hair dryer on the desk. And she distinctly remembered sliding her suitcase under the bed.

But wait, maybe she was just being paranoid. Hadn't she pulled the suitcase out again when she'd taken out the T-shirt and jeans she'd worn to the disco? And how could she be so sure she didn't leave her robe and dryer where they were now? It was true that she wasn't normally that sloppy, but she'd had her mind on other things—namely, Nick—as she'd gotten ready to go to the disco.

Kelly began to breathe a little easier. Maybe she was mistaken. Maybe because the door wouldn't lock, and she was so convinced she was going to find something wrong, she imagined she had.

Or maybe she was just tired. It had been a long day. Kelly wedged the chair under the door and pushed the desk up behind it. Then she undressed and got into bed. In no time at all she was asleep.

The next morning Kelly opened her eyes and stared at her alarm clock. *Eight fifty-five!* It couldn't be! She'd set it for eight A.M. Why hadn't it gone off?

She had no time to wonder as she quickly threw on a bathing suit and hurried down to the pool. The other lifeguards had already gotten there. As Kelly pushed through the glass doors into the indoor pool, she saw Tiffany spring off the diving board and do a beautiful double flip. Kelly looked around to see if Nick was there, but he wasn't.

"Hey, Kelly!"

Eric. When Kelly turned to greet him, she was surprised. Eric was short, but he had a very well-developed body. He must have spent a lot of time lifting weights.

"Hi, Eric," she said.

Eric flexed his arms and puffed his chest out. Kelly could see that he wanted to make sure she admired his muscles. "I thought you would have been here by now," he said.

"My alarm clock didn't go off," Kelly explained. "Come on, let's get everyone together."

A few moments later, the lifeguards stood in a semicircle around Kelly. In addition to Eric, Tiffany, and Chip, the guy Kelly had danced with a few times the night before, there was a short girl with black hair, named Claire.

Kelly introduced herself and talked about how she wanted to run the lifeguard crew. They discussed safety rules and schedules and days off. The reason they needed five guards for two pools was that the lifeguards had to rotate positions frequently and cover for each other on their days off.

Kelly was just finishing up her talk when Martin arrived. She dismissed the other guards, who went off to man the lifeguard chairs and do other chores.

"Sleep well?" Martin asked.

"Like a log," Kelly said.

Was it Kelly's imagination, or did Martin look a little surprised?

"Well, I came down because there are a couple of things I need to show you," he said. He led Kelly through the glass doors that led to the outdoor pool. Past the outdoor pool and across a patch of grass, they came to a small, garage-size building. Martin took out a key and unlocked the door.

"This, as you probably know, is the heating and filtration plant," Martin said as they stepped inside. The building felt warm and smelled strongly of chlorine. A large filtering system in the middle of the floor hummed loudly.

"The heat's controlled by a thermostat on the wall by the indoor pool, but once a week you have to have one of the guards clean out and backwash the filter," Martin said. He pointed to a red switch on the filtering system. "This is the emergency on-off switch, if you ever have to turn the filtering system off."

"Why would I have to turn it off?" Kelly asked.

"Well, suppose there was a leak somewhere and the water level in the pools dropped," Martin said. "You'd have to turn it off, or the whole filtration system could burn out. The pool is one of the inn's key attractions. It's very important that it's always safe and well-maintained."

Martin also showed her where the large plastic jugs of chlorine were stored. "We use liquid chlorine," he said. "After testing the water with a special kit, you'll know how much to put in. You'll probably have someone add it about every four days."

Next he pointed to a blue plastic bucket filled with blue crystals. "This is the declouder. If for any reason the water gets cloudy, throw a cup of this in. It'll clear up in no time."

When he was finished, he locked the door and gave Kelly two keys. One was for the little building. The other was for the lifeguard office beside the indoor pool.

"It's best if you hold on to these keys and don't make any copies," Martin said. "The storage building and the office are strictly off-limits to hotel guests. If any of the lifeguards needs to use a key, they have to borrow it from you and return it when they're done."

Kelly said she understood, then went back to see how the other guards were doing. It was turning out to be a hot, sunny day, and many of the inn's guests were starting to set up lounges on the terrace around the outdoor pool.

The only people using the indoor pool were a pack of younger kids doing cannonballs off the diving board and having water fights.

Since everything looked as though it was under control, Kelly thought it might be a good time to take a look at the lifeguard office. She walked across to the far side of the indoor pool, slid her key into the office door, and pushed it open.

The lights were on inside the office. The room was tiny and windowless. The air was stuffy and hot. A tall file cabinet stood against one wall, across from a desk and a couple of chairs. Kelly immediately noticed that several of the file cabinet drawers were pulled open, as well as the drawers in the desk. She was just reaching to close them when someone grabbed her from behind.

A hand slid around her mouth and muffled her cry for help.

Chapter 5

Kelly struggled, but she couldn't get away. The person holding her was strong and kept a tight grip.

"Promise me you won't scream," he hissed.

Kelly tried to say something, but her words were distorted by the stranger's hand.

"Promise?" he whispered again.

Kelly nodded, and he let go. She spun around and gasped. *It was Nick!*

"Why did you do that?" she asked angrily.

"Shush!" He pressed his finger to his lips. "You promised."

Kelly tried to regain her composure. "You had no right to grab me like that. I was terrified. What's the matter with you?"

"I didn't want you to scream," Nick said.

"Well, you almost gave me a heart attack," Kelly said. "What are you doing in here, anyway?"

Nick slid his hands into his pockets and stared at the floor. "I can't tell you."

"Oh, really?" Kelly said. "Then maybe I ought to tell someone I found you in here. Guests aren't supposed to be in the lifeguard's office."

Nick looked up and fixed his steady gaze on her. "Please don't tell anyone."

"Why shouldn't I?" Kelly asked.

"Because," Nick said, "I'm asking you not to."

"Then I suggest you tell *me*," Kelly said.

Nick shook his head. Kelly just stared at him. "You have to tell me something."

"Do I?" Nick asked.

Kelly sighed. She knew that in a way he was right. He didn't *have* to tell her anything, and she still probably wouldn't tell anyone she had found him in the lifeguard office.

"You weren't doing anything wrong, were you?" Kelly asked. "I mean, you weren't trying to steal anything."

Nick shook his head.

"How long have you been here?" Kelly asked.

"Here in this room, or here at the inn?" Nick replied.

"At the inn."

"Four days."

"Where are your parents?"

"Not around," Nick said.

Kelly shook her head. "Eric was right. You really are a mystery man."

32

Nick smiled slightly and leaned against the edge of the desk. Seeing that made Kelly feel a little more comfortable.

"You're a good dancer," he said.

"Uh, thank you." Kelly felt self-conscious.

"Maybe tonight you and I will get to dance," he said.

"What about Tiffany?" Kelly asked.

"What about her?"

"It looked as though you and she are together."

"I hardly know her," Nick said.

"I think she likes you," Kelly said.

"I think Eric likes *you*," Nick replied.

"Well, the feeling is definitely *not* mutual."

Nick smiled. "I know what you mean." He slid off the desk. "I'm sorry if I scared you before." It looked as if he was going to leave.

"Wait," Kelly said. "I'd really feel better if you'd just tell me why you were in here."

"I can't," Nick said. "Maybe someday. Not now."

"Then just tell me how you got in," Kelly said.

Nick reached into his pocket and pulled out a plastic card. It looked like a credit card, except that it was badly bent and creased.

"So?" Kelly said.

"I wedged it between the lock and the door frame," Nick said.

"Can you get into any room you want?" Kelly asked.

"Almost," Nick said. He turned toward the door, then stopped and looked back at her.

"Promise me you won't tell anyone," he said. He held her with a steady, intense gaze. Kelly felt goose bumps run down her arms. "Considerate it a favor to me," Nick said. "I'll pay you back someday, okay?"

"All right," Kelly said.

"I owe you one." Nick smiled slightly. "I eat dinner with the lifeguards at the same table every night. Usually around seven, after the pool closes. Will I see you there?"

"Do you want to?" Kelly asked.

"You bet." Nick winked and went out, pulling the door closed behind him.

Kelly spent the rest of the day getting to know the pool and the facilities. She swam in both the indoor and outdoor pools and looked for the "blind spots" where it would be hard for a lifeguard to see someone in trouble. The pool water was clear and very refreshing, despite all the chemicals they had to put in it for health reasons.

She went over the safety equipment—the long hook the lifeguards used to pull people out of the water, the floats, and the body splint for people with neck injuries. Everything looked as though it was in good order. Then she did the late shift on lifeguard duty at the outdoor pool. She hadn't seen Nick since that encounter in the office, and she hoped he might come out to the pool for a late-afternoon swim. But he didn't.

Unfortunately, Eric did.

"Hi, how's it going?" he asked.

Kelly looked down from the lifeguard chair. "Okay, how about you?"

"Okay," Eric said. "Hey, want to bet I can't do twenty-five chin-ups?"

"Not really."

Eric frowned. "Come on. I bet I'm the only guy in this whole place that can do that many."

"I believe you," Kelly said.

"Want to see?" Eric grabbed a bar under the lifeguard chair and proceeded to do twenty-five chin-ups.

"Pretty good, huh?" he gasped when he was finished. His muscular body was covered with sweat.

"Very impressive," Kelly said noncommittally.

"Now how about a hundred push-ups?"

"I'd love to see you do it, Eric, but I'm afraid I have to watch the pool."

"Okay, maybe later," Eric said. "I think I'll go for a run. I usually do five miles in under forty minutes. That's less than eight minutes a mile."

"Really?" Kelly pretended to be interested.

Eric waved good-bye and jogged away. Kelly shook her head and smiled to herself. Despite all his muscles, Eric was a total geek.

When the pool closed at six o'clock, Kelly

walked back to her room with Claire, the small girl with black hair.

"So how do you like it here so far?" Claire asked as they waited for the elevator.

"It seems pretty nice," Kelly said. "How do you like it?"

"It's okay," Claire said. "I just hope I can do it, you know?"

"Do what?" Kelly asked uncertainly.

"Well, you know, save someone if I have to," Claire said.

Kelly tried to hide her surprise. "You are a certified lifeguard, aren't you?"

"Oh, sure," Claire said. "But you know how those courses are. The people you practice on aren't actually drowning. It's not as if you ever have the experience of *really* saving someone. I mean, until you really save someone."

"I'm sure you'll be okay," Kelly said.

The elevator came and they got in.

"Have you ever done it?" Claire asked.

"Saved someone?"

Claire nodded.

"To tell you the truth, I haven't," Kelly said. "It's not something that happens a lot in pools. But with the safety equipment they have here, I don't think you have to worry."

Claire nodded. Kelly had the feeling Claire was the kind of person who would worry anyway. The elevator stopped at the third floor and they got out.

"Did anyone tell you that the lifeguards usually eat together at seven?" Claire asked.

"Uh-huh."

Claire stopped outside the door of the room she shared with Tiffany. "So I guess I'll see you then."

"Why don't I stop by your room in an hour, and we'll go together?" Kelly asked.

"Okay, great," Claire said. She went into her room and Kelly continued down the hall.

Kelly stopped outside her door, hoping that Sebastian had fixed the lock by now. She pushed on the door, and it swung open.

Disappointed, Kelly stepped into the room and turned on the light. Once again she had the weird feeling that something had changed since she had been there that morning. When she looked around, though, nothing seemed out of place. And yet she had a nagging sensation, as if everything had been moved just a fraction of an inch.

Like the night before, Kelly wedged the chair against the door and pushed the desk against it. Then she locked herself in her bathroom and took a long, hot shower.

At seven o'clock she knocked on Claire's door, and the two of them went down to the dining room. The lifeguards were all sitting at a large round table. Nick was also there, sitting next to Tiffany. When Kelly came in, Eric quickly jumped up.

37

"I've been saving this seat for you," he said.

Kelly rolled her eyes as she sat down next to him. Claire took the only other chair available at the table.

Kelly heard a loud *crack!*

Suddenly Claire disappeared.

Chapter 6

Everybody instantly jumped up and ran around the table to Claire. She was lying on the floor with a shocked look on her face. Nick quickly reached down and helped her up.

"Are you okay?" he asked.

"I think so." Shaking a little, Claire stood up and brushed herself off. "Nothing like that's ever happened to me before."

"It's a clear indication that you have to lose some weight," Eric said.

Everybody frowned at him.

"Hey, it was just a joke," he explained. "I mean, does Claire look like she needs to lose weight?"

"No, but it still isn't funny," Tiffany said.

"Well, *excuuuuse* me," Eric said.

Meanwhile, Nick picked up the broken chair. "Hey, look at this," he said, showing everyone the place where the leg had snapped. "It looks as though the leg was sawed almost completely through. It wouldn't have taken much weight at all to make it split."

"I guess it's just someone's idea of a bad joke," said Chip.

Nick went to get Claire another chair. "I checked this one," he said. "All the legs are sturdy."

"Thanks." Claire carefully sat down again.

Everyone else joined her at the table. Eric immediately turned to Kelly. "So how'd you like your first day?"

"It was fine," Kelly said.

"Anything interesting, exciting, or unusual happen?"

Kelly caught Nick's eye for a second. Almost imperceptibly, he shook his head.

"Nope," Kelly said.

Dinner was served buffet style. Kelly wasn't surprised when Tiffany followed Nick to the food table. When Kelly got up to go, Eric followed. But when she stopped at the salad bar, Eric went ahead. Kelly was sprinkling croutons on her salad when she heard Nick say, "Vegetarian?"

She looked up and saw him smiling at her from across the salad bar.

"Not really," she said. "Where's Tiffany?"

"Getting a hamburger," Nick said. "Don't go to the disco after dinner."

"Why not?" Kelly asked, surprised.

"Just don't," he said. "Wait for me in your room."

Kelly felt a tingling sensation. She thought Nick was being awfully forward, but she wasn't going to argue.

"I'm on the third floor," Kelly said.

"Yes, I know. Last room at the end of the hall."

Kelly stared at him, shocked. She wanted to ask how he knew that, but Nick had already moved to the next table.

Eric, of course, was extremely disappointed after dinner when Kelly said she wanted to go back to her room and write a letter to a friend.

"Why don't you write it tomorrow?"

"I work tomorrow," Kelly said.

"I'll tell you what," Eric said. "I'll cover for you tomorrow while you write the letter."

"That's very nice of you," Kelly said. "But I really want to write it tonight."

"Okay, okay," Eric said. "Go write it, but how about coming down to the disco when you're finished?"

"I probably won't have time," Kelly said.

"Oh, come on," Eric said. "How long does it take to write a letter?"

The conversation was becoming silly. Kelly said she'd come to the disco if she finished the letter in time, even though she had no intention of doing so.

A few minutes later Kelly let herself into her room and wedged the chair against the door. She actually did want to write a letter, and got out a pad of paper and a pen. She wanted to write to Tom, the boy she'd dated all winter. Tom was one of the top athletes in her school and one of the smartest students as well. He was very popular and good-looking, and Kelly's friends never stopped reminding her how lucky she was to be going out with him.

Kelly wrote *Dear Tom,* and then stared at the blank notepad for a long time. Tom was everything a girl could want, but . . . well, he wasn't Nick. There was just something special about Nick. Something about the spark in his eyes and the mysterious smile on his lips both thrilled and frightened Kelly. Tom was easy to boss around. He'd do almost anything Kelly told him to do. On the other hand, Kelly found it hard to say no to Nick.

There was a knock on her door.

"Who is it?"

"Nick."

Kelly felt a shiver run down her spine and goose bumps rise on her arms. She'd never once let Tom into her bedroom at home, even after she'd known him for more than a year. Now here she was, letting Nick into her room. Nick, whom she'd known for only a day.

She put away the notepad, then stood up and

pulled the chair away from the door. "Come on in."

Nick stepped into the room. He was wearing a faded polo shirt, jeans, and deck shoes. Kelly closed the door behind him, but didn't wedge the chair against it. Instead she gave it to Nick to sit on while she sat cross-legged on the bed.

"We escaped," she said, feeling nervous.

"Yes." Nick sat down and aimed his steady gaze at her.

"How did you get away from Tiffany?"

"I told her my back hurt and I was going to get a massage in the spa."

Kelly grinned. "Obviously something she couldn't join you for."

"I would have welcomed it." Nick grinned back, then added, "Just kidding."

Kelly's stomach was starting to feel tight. She knew that soon it would start to hurt. He made her nervous, but in an exciting way.

"Why did you want to see me?" she asked.

"It isn't obvious?"

"Not really."

Nick tilted the chair back and balanced on the rear two legs. "I know I must seem mysterious in some ways, but there's no mystery where you're concerned. I really like you, Kelly."

"You like me, but you still won't tell me why you were in the lifeguard office today," Kelly said.

"It has nothing to do with you," Nick said. "Believe me."

Kelly pressed her fingers to her lips. She thought for a moment. She did like Nick, but she had to admit that he was acting pretty weird. "You're here without your parents, but you don't really seem to be here to have fun. It's like you're on some kind of mission or something."

The front legs of the chair banged down, and Nick stood up. "I want to be here with you," he said. "But I can't stay if you keep trying to figure me out."

"Sorry," Kelly said. "I guess it's my natural curiosity."

Nick nodded and went to stare out her window. "Nice view," he said. "Even at night."

"You mean the pool?" Kelly asked.

"Uh-huh."

"Martin said that was why he gave me this room. So I could keep an eye on the pool day and night."

"What do you think of Martin?" Nick asked.

"I'm not sure," Kelly said. "I think maybe he's a little strange."

Nick nodded and gazed out the window. Suddenly he frowned. "Hey, I think you better look at this."

Kelly got up and went to the window. At first glance she couldn't see anything wrong. "What?"

"There," Nick said. "Past the outdoor pool."

Kelly cupped her hands against the glass and stared into the darkness. It was a clear night, and the moon and stars were out. There appeared to be a large puddle of water between the outdoor pool and the storage building where the filtering system was. Kelly thought she could see the reflection of the moon and the stars in the water.

"Maybe we should go have a look," she said.

A minute later Kelly and Nick left the inn and walked quickly around the outdoor pool. Even before she got to the little building, Kelly knew something was wrong. The level of the outdoor pool was almost two feet lower than it should have been.

The grassy patch of lawn between the outdoor pool and the filtration building was flooded like a lake.

"A pipe must have broken," Kelly said.

"Should we get help?" Nick asked.

"Yes." Kelly bent down and pulled off her shoes. "But first I have to turn off the filtration system before it burns out."

Kelly stepped into the huge puddle. The ground beneath her feet felt soft and the grass felt spongy. As she slogged toward the building, the water got deeper and the ground felt squishy with deep mud. Kelly guessed she was nearing the place where the water from the broken pipe was seeping up to the surface. Suddenly her right foot hit something hard, like a tree branch or a pipe.

Kelly tried to step around it, but her ankle had gotten caught. She plunged her hands into the water and reached down to free herself. The thing around her ankle was strange and hard—not at all like a tree branch. As Kelly felt around it, she had a sudden weird fear of what it might be.

A shiver of terror shot up her spine.

"*Help!*" she cried.

Chapter 7

"What? What's wrong?" Nick called and started to splash through the water toward her.

"*Oh, help! Please help me!*" Kelly shrieked. She couldn't believe what she thought she had felt still gripping her ankle. It felt like—but no, it was impossible. Totally impossible. It was bony and cold. It was snaked tightly around her ankle, its sharp, jointed grip digging into her skin.

Oh, God . . .

"Nick!" Kelly staggered in the wet, muddy puddle, desperately trying not to lose her balance as she struggled to wrench her foot free. But no matter how hard she fought against it, Kelly couldn't pull her ankle loose.

Nick was only a few feet away now, splashing toward her. "Are you okay? What's wrong?"

Suddenly Kelly felt her ankle pull free.

A second later Nick grabbed her around the waist. "What? What was it?"

Kelly's heart was beating so hard she could barely breathe. "Get me to the storage building," she gasped.

With Nick helping her, Kelly managed to stagger into the filtration building and flick the emergency switch to off. Then she collapsed to the floor and began to sob.

"What was it, Kelly?" Nick asked, crouching beside her and holding her shoulders. "What happened?"

Kelly tried to talk, but she was panting so hard she couldn't get the words out. Her stomach churned violently, and she had to breathe deeply to keep from getting sick.

"You're hyperventilating," Nick said. "Try to relax. You have to calm down."

He put his arms around her and hugged her tightly. "I don't know what happened out there, but nothing's going to hurt you, Kelly. I promise you, you're okay."

Kelly's gasps gradually slowed. Her lungs throbbed painfully from breathing so hard. She reached for one of Nick's arms and clung to it.

"You still haven't told me what happened," Nick said.

"As . . . as I was walking through the water, I . . . I felt something rub against my ankle," Kelly said with a sob. "My ankle felt caught. I thought it was a branch or a tree root or something, but it wasn't."

"What was it?"

Kelly stared up at him. She knew it would sound crazy. It *was* crazy. But she had felt it herself, had touched those bony fingers. . . . "It was a skeleton," she whispered. "A skeleton's hand."

Nick stared back at her. "You're joking."

"I swear I'm not," Kelly gasped.

"You're sure?" Nick asked. "I mean, that's pretty wild."

"I felt it, Nick," Kelly insisted. "I reached down with my hands and felt it. I could feel the fingers and the knuckles."

The memory of it sent another shiver through her.

"Couldn't it have been a forked branch or something?" Nick asked.

"No, it wasn't," Kelly said. "You have to believe me. You'll see. Now that the filter system's stopped running, the water will drain away. You'll see when the water's gone."

They heard voices outside, then splashing sounds. A second later the door to the filtration building opened, and Martin and Sebastian came in. Martin stared at the filtration system and then turned to Kelly.

"You turned it off?"

Kelly nodded and wiped her eyes with her sleeve.

"Good work," Martin said. "The pool lost a lot

49

of water. If the filter had run much longer, it probably would have burned out."

"What do you think is wrong?" Nick asked.

"Probably a leak in the filtering system," Sebastian said. "One of the pipes that runs from the pool to the filter must have ruptured."

Nick glanced at Kelly, then back at Sebastian. "What would cause a pipe to rupture like that? I mean, those things are buried deep in the ground, aren't they?"

"Not all that deep. A couple feet, maybe. But the ground moves," Sebastian said. "Not like an earthquake or anything. Just gradually. Things settle."

"Was there ever a graveyard here?" Kelly asked abruptly.

"Here?" Sebastian frowned, then stared at Martin for a moment. "No, I don't think so. Not that I know of, at least. Anyway, I don't think they would have built a pool over a graveyard."

"What if it was really old?" Kelly asked. "Like, here long before this place was built?"

"That could be, but they still would have turned something up when they put in the pool," Sebastian said. "Why are you asking?"

Kelly was about to explain when she noticed Nick out of the corner of her eye. He was shaking his head in the same almost imperceptible way he'd shaken it earlier. For some reason he didn't want her to tell Martin and Sebastian what she'd told him.

"Oh, uh, no real reason," Kelly quickly said. "I'm just curious about this place."

Sebastian glanced again at Martin.

"I'm glad you were keeping an eye on the pool," Martin said. "You probably saved the inn a lot of money. Now we'll go call the maintenance company."

He and Sebastian left. Kelly turned to Nick. "Why didn't you want me to tell them about the skeleton's hand?"

"I don't know," Nick said. "It just didn't feel right. We better go."

Kelly got up, but when she got to the door of the little building she suddenly stopped. A lot of the water had already drained away outside, but the ground was still soft and wet.

"I can't walk back through that," she said.

"Okay," Nick said, taking her hand. "No problem."

He led her around the flooded area, and they walked back into the inn and up to her room. Kelly stopped outside her door and looked up at him.

"I wish I knew you better," she said.

"Why?"

"Because then I'd ask you to stay on my floor tonight. I'm pretty freaked out. I could use the company."

Nick smiled. "Just lock the door. You'll be fine."

"I can't," Kelly said. "The lock's broken. Sebastian was supposed to fix it, but he hasn't yet."

"Do you want to come stay in my room?" Nick asked. "I really wouldn't mind sleeping on the floor."

"I'd better not," Kelly said reluctantly. "If I push the chair against the door no one will be able to get in. I'll be all right."

"If you wanted, I could stay with you until you fell asleep," Nick said.

"No," Kelly said. "I'm feeling a lot better now that we're inside. I doubt there any skeletons in my room. Anyway, thanks for saving me." She tried to smile bravely, then pulled open the door and started to go in.

"Wait," Nick said. Kelly turned toward him.

"I know what we should do," Nick said. "Let's get up early tomorrow morning and go look for whatever it was that grabbed you."

Kelly's eyes went wide. "No way. I'm never going near that place again."

"Look, I'll be with you," Nick said. "I promise nothing will happen to you. But it's important to find out if something's really there. If you don't, you'll walk around with doubts. And believe me, that's something you can't live with."

Chapter 8

The next morning Kelly woke to hear someone knocking softly on her door. She looked at her alarm clock. It was six thirty.

"Who is it?" she asked with a yawn.

"Nick. I said I'd get you, remember?"

"Oh, right." Kelly sat up and rubbed her eyes. "Give me a minute."

She got up and went into the bathroom. She still didn't understand why Nick wanted to go back and search for the skeletal hand. The whole idea gave her the creeps.

After dressing quickly in shorts and a T-shirt, she met Nick outside in the hall.

"How'd you sleep?" he asked as they walked toward the elevator.

"Amazingly well, all things considered," Kelly replied.

"No nightmares about skeletons reaching up

out of the ground and grabbing you, huh?" Nick kidded.

"I'm not *that* bad," Kelly said with a smirk.

A few moments later they walked out onto the terrace around the outdoor pool. The sky was clear, and the air felt fresh and cool. Ahead of them, the grassy patch of ground between the pool and the filtering building was wet and still muddy. Kelly stopped near the edge.

"I think I'll wait here," she said.

"Okay." Nick bent down and pulled off his deck shoes and socks. Then he rolled up the bottoms of his jeans. Kelly hugged herself and shivered at the memory of what had happened the night before.

She watched as Nick canvassed the whole muddy area carefully. He even found a stick, which he used to work through the muddier places. Finally he looked up at her and shook his head. "There's nothing here."

"There has to be," Kelly said. "I mean, it's not exactly like a skeleton can walk around."

"You saw how I just searched for it," Nick said. "I don't see how I could have missed anything."

Without thinking, Kelly pulled off her tennis shoes. She hated the sensation of stepping onto the muddy, slippery grass, but she had to prove to Nick and herself that she wasn't imagining things.

For the next twenty minutes, Kelly covered every inch of the soggy patch of ground. Not only was she unable to find the skeleton's hand, but she couldn't find a branch or a stick or anything else that she might have mistaken for that hand.

"Do you think someone got here before us?" Kelly asked.

"I thought of that," Nick said. "But when we first got out here, I didn't see anyone else's footprints."

"I don't get it," Kelly said. "I *know* I felt something. My ankle was totally caught. I reached down . . . felt it with my hands . . . how could I be wrong? I'm sure it was a skeleton. A skeleton's hand was holding my ankle," she said firmly.

"Come over here," Nick said.

Kelly joined him. Nick was standing over a muddy, funnel-shaped hole in the ground.

"This must be right over where the pipe broke," he said. "Look." He took his stick and stuck it down into the hole. Kelly could see that if Nick let go, the stick would drop down and disappear.

"You think it could have fallen down that hole?" Kelly asked.

"I can't figure out what else could have happened," Nick said. "You're right, it couldn't have just disappeared."

Kelly squatted down and gave the funnel-shaped hole a closer look. "Let me see something," she said, reaching up for the stick. Nick handed it to her, and she started to scrape away the mud on the sides of the hole. Suddenly she uncovered something. It looked like a string of small round white beads with letters on them. She picked it up and rubbed the mud off the beads.

"What's it say?" Nick asked.

"It's someone's name," Kelly said. "Laura."

"Back again?" a voice suddenly asked behind them.

Kelly turned and saw Martin standing at the edge of the muddy ground.

"Uh, Kelly thought she dropped something last night," Nick said quickly. "We came back to look for it."

"Well, you'll have to clear out now," Martin said. "We've got a repair crew coming in to fix the leak."

Kelly slipped the beads into her pocket, and she and Nick walked back toward Martin.

"We're closing the pool for the day," Martin said. "Hopefully it won't take longer than that to fix. The guests don't like it when they can't use the pool."

"What does the repair crew have to do?" Kelly asked.

"Dig up the pipe and replace the broken part," Martin said.

"Dig it up?" Kelly repeated, interested.

Martin nodded. "You'll have to put up signs saying the pool is closed for the day."

"Okay." Kelly and Nick got their shoes and started back toward the inn.

"You think the repair crew is going to find something they don't expect?" Nick asked when they were out of Martin's earshot.

"I don't *think* so," Kelly replied. "I *know* so."

Chapter 9

"Hey, what happened to the water?" Eric asked. The lifeguards had gathered beside the indoor pool, which was almost empty.

Kelly explained how the pipe to the filter had broken. Outside they could see a crew of workmen gathered on the muddy patch of ground between the outdoor pool and the filtration building. They were bringing in a small backhoe to dig up the broken pipe.

"They had to drain the pool before they can fix the pipe," Kelly explained. "They figure it will take all day."

"Then it's a day off for us," Tiffany said.

"Basically," Kelly said. "But first we have to make some signs saying the pools are closed. And we better rope off both pools in case someone doesn't notice the signs."

"Yeah, I can just see it," Eric said. He waved

his arms and started to run toward the edge of the indoor pool like a little kid. "Hey, Mom! Watch me do a cannonball! Then . . . *splat!*"

The other lifeguards grinned.

"Okay, guys," Kelly said. She didn't think Eric's joke was so funny. "Let's get to work."

They made the signs and roped off the pools. Nick showed up just as the lifeguards were finishing. Kelly saw him walking toward her, but Tiffany intercepted him.

"Nick, since I have the day off, would you like to do something?" she said.

Nick glanced at Kelly and caught her eye. Then he turned back to Tiffany. "Uh, sure. I just need to talk to Kelly for a second."

He stepped close to Kelly and spoke in a low voice. "How are you going to know if they find anything?"

"I thought I'd pull a lounge out to the edge of the terrace and get some sun," Kelly answered.

Nick smiled. "Good idea. See you later," he said.

Kelly watched him walk toward Tiffany. Someone tapped her on the shoulder, and she turned to find Eric behind her.

"So now what?" Eric asked.

"You can take the rest of the day off," Kelly said.

"What are you gonna do?" Eric asked.

"Me? I thought I'd just get my CD player and lie in the sun."

"Great," Eric said. "Let's go. I've got some great CDs in my room."

Kelly instantly regretted telling Eric her plans. Unfortunately, it was too late to back out now—she was trapped with him for the day. They rode the elevator up to the third floor and went to their rooms. Kelly pushed her door open and stopped short. Once again, the room seemed slightly different. Looking around, she could see that nothing had been taken. Then she saw the note.

Sitting on her pillow was a torn piece of paper. *STAY AWAY FROM THE POOL*, the handwriting said. Kelly tore the paper up and threw it in the wastebasket. It was a stupid joke by one of the other lifeguards. Kelly didn't see the humor in it, though. In the back of her mind she couldn't help wondering if the warning was serious. She shrugged the idea off. The weirdness at the New Arcadia was just making her nervous.

Kelly got her CD player from the desk drawer. She decided that before she went to the patio she would pay a visit to Sebastian to find out why her lock hadn't been fixed yet. As she shut her door, Eric came out of his room with a small stack of CDs in his hands.

"Hey, perfect timing." He grinned.

"Almost," Kelly said. "I just have to make a stop at the front desk."

"Okay. Let's go."

"Uh, I might be a while," Kelly said. "Why don't I meet you on the patio?"

"Oh, uh, sure."

"Could you do me a favor and take my CD player with you?" Kelly asked.

"No sweat," Eric said.

They got out of the elevator and Eric turned right to go toward the pool. Kelly turned left and headed for the front desk. Sarah, the girl with red hair, was there.

Kelly stopped and stared at Sarah in disbelief. The girl was wearing a gold cross on a gold chain around her neck. It looked exactly like the gold cross and chain Kelly had put in her jewelry bag and left in the safe.

"Can I help you?" Sarah asked.

Kelly had no idea what to say. Was it possible that Sarah had the same exact cross as she?

"Uh, I was wondering if I could get my jewelry bag out of the safe," Kelly said.

"Oh, uh, just a minute." Sarah went through the door and into the manager's office. A few moments later she returned to the desk. "The manager's not here right now. He's the only one who knows the combination to the safe."

Kelly stared at her, wondering if she was lying. If Sarah had stolen her necklace, she wouldn't be so dumb to wear it in broad daylight, would she? "Well, do you know where I can find Sebastian?"

"Why do you need him?" Sarah asked rudely.

"I have to talk to him about something," Kelly said, feeling a little uncomfortable. Why was it any of Sarah's business? It seemed as if the red-haired girl was trying to antagonize her.

"He's probably down at the boathouse," Sarah said.

Without a word Kelly headed toward the lake. She followed the signs and went down a trail that came to a cliff. In front of her were some stairs leading down to the boathouse and a dock lined with sailboats and Jet Skis. Kelly went down the stairs and walked out to the boathouse.

The door was open, and she stepped inside. She could hear the sound of sawing and of someone humming to himself. Following the sound, she went into a small workshop. Tools were hanging from pegboards on the walls, and Sebastian was standing at a worktable. He had his back to her and appeared to be sawing something.

Kelly was about to say something when she noticed what he was sawing.

A chair. A chair just like the one that had broken when Claire sat on it.

Sebastian was sawing through one of the legs.

Chapter 10

Kelly watched in amazement as Sebastian sawed almost all the way through the leg and then stopped.

"There," he said with a smile. "That ought to do it."

He picked up the chair and turned. When he saw Kelly, his jaw dropped and a look of shock crossed his face.

"What are you doing here?" he asked.

"I came down here to ask you about my lock," Kelly replied. "But now that I'm here, I want to know why you sawed through that chair leg."

Sebastian looked flustered. "Oh, uh, well, that was just the first step, really. You see, I'm actually fixing it. Uh, reinforcing it is what I'm doing."

"Reinforcing it?" Kelly had her doubts.

"Right," Sebastian said.

"You know, last night Claire had a nasty fall because the chair she'd been sitting on had had its leg sawed partway through. Weird, huh?" Kelly said coolly.

"Well, er, it's possible I put one back by accident without finishing the job," Sebastian said, scratching his head. "I am kind of forgetful. So, uh, how can I help you?"

Kelly just stared at him. Like Sarah at the front desk, Sebastian had come up with explanations, but Kelly didn't really believe them. But how could she prove he was lying?

"I came by to see if you'd fixed my lock," she said.

"Lock?" Sebastian rubbed his chin and looked puzzled.

"To the door of my room," Kelly said.

"Oh, right, *that* lock." He shook his head. "Nope, I haven't."

"Is there a problem?" Kelly asked.

"Oh, no, I've just been busy taking care of other things," Sebastian said. "I'm sure I can get to it first thing tomorrow morning."

"Well, I'd really appreciate it," Kelly said uncomfortably. "It's been two days already, and I really don't like not being able to lock my door."

"I understand," Sebastian said. "Like I said, it'll be done first thing tomorrow."

Kelly left the boathouse, but she was really disturbed. Sebastian said he'd been too busy to fix her lock. But what had he been busy doing? Sawing chair legs?

Eric was waiting for her on the terrace. He'd set out two lounges for them. It was midmorning, and the lounges faced the sun. But Kelly moved hers so that it faced the men working on the broken pipe.

"What are you doing?" Eric asked.

"I want to be able to watch them," Kelly said.

"I guess you take your job pretty seriously."

Kelly smiled, but didn't reply.

Eric turned his lounge around so that it faced the same direction as hers. He took out one of his CDs.

"The Spin Doctors," he said. "Ever heard of them?"

Kelly shook her head. Thirty feet away, the workmen had begun to dig into the ground with the backhoe.

"Well, they're great." Eric slipped the CD into Kelly's CD player. "Did you know your batteries were dead?"

Kelly looked down and frowned. "I just replaced them. It should work."

"Look at your battery light." Eric pointed at a small red light that was barely glowing. "Your batteries are completely drained."

"That can't be," Kelly said. "I just put new ones

in a few days ago. I've hardly used it since then."

"Well, the battery light doesn't lie," Eric said.

Kelly shook her head and sighed. It seemed as though nothing worked around here. Door locks, chairs, swimming pools, CD players . . . *And she'd only been there two days!*

She wondered if someone had been using her CD player. They could have easily taken it from her room. Maybe it was the person who had left her that note.

For the next half hour, Kelly watched as the big curved claw of the backhoe scooped away the earth. Unfortunately, she also had to listen to Eric drone on and on about his physical prowess.

"I think the great thing about being small and strong is that I'm a lot quicker than most people think," Eric bragged. "I mean, put me up against some guy who's six inches taller and weighs fifty pounds more. He may be stronger and able to hit harder, but that doesn't mean he's going to be able to land a punch. You understand? Uh, Kelly?"

"Huh?" Kelly turned and stared blankly at him. She'd been daydreaming about the moment when the workers found that skeleton.

"I asked if you understood what I was talking about," Eric said.

"You're quicker," Kelly said mechanically.

"Yeah, exactly," Eric said. "So even if the guy is

bigger and stronger, he probably won't be able to tag me."

Suddenly Kelly heard a shout. A workman was standing in the hole, waving his arms at his co-workers. "Hey, look at this!"

Chapter 11

Kelly jumped to her feet and hurried toward the hole.

"Hey!" Eric shouted behind her. "Where are you going?"

Kelly didn't reply. A couple of workmen were already standing at the edge of the hole when she got there. She joined them and looked down. A moment later Eric caught up to her.

"What's the deal?" he asked.

The workman was standing in a puddle of muddy water at the bottom of the hole. As Kelly watched, he reached down into the murky water and lifted something up.

Kelly held her breath as she tried to get a glimpse of the object. She let her breath out and gasped.

It was only a broken piece of pipe.

Kelly was very disappointed and started to turn away.

"Ever see anything like it?" the worker asked the others.

"Nope," said one of the men.

"Pretty strange," said another.

Kelly stopped and turned back toward them. "What's so strange about it?"

"That's four-inch cast-iron pipe," the man said. "You could run a tank over it and it wouldn't break. The piece he's holding was broken clear through in two places. You have to wonder what could have possibly done that."

The man's words meant little to Kelly. All she knew was that they'd dug clear down to the pipe and hadn't found the skeleton. What could have happened to it? Was she just crazy, after all?

Kelly turned back toward the terrace.

"Hey, Kelly." Eric jogged to catch up to her. "The guy said it would probably only take a couple of hours to put a new section of pipe in. He figures they'll be able to fill the hole in by this afternoon. Then they can start refilling the pool. It'll be ready by tomorrow morning."

Kelly nodded, but she wasn't listening to Eric. What could have happened to the skeleton? How could it have disappeared? She and Nick were the only ones who knew about it, and *she* certainly hadn't taken it.

She got back to the lounge and sat down again. Eric sat down beside her.

"Did I tell you that I placed second in the

county triathlon?" Eric began. "I would have finished first, except that . . ."

For the rest of the afternoon, Kelly sat in the sun and listened to more stories of Eric's great athletic exploits. After a while, she hardly heard him anymore. It was like highway noise—you grow so used to it that you forget you live by the highway.

All day Kelly wondered about the skeleton. She kept telling herself that Nick wouldn't have done anything with it. Or if he had, he would have told her. But as the day passed, her doubts grew. She hardly knew him. She already knew he was keeping secrets from her. Why should she trust him?

"Well, I guess it's almost time for dinner," Eric said as the sun began to drop in the western sky. "You want to go inside?"

Kelly sat up. "Could you excuse me for a second?"

"Uh, okay," Eric said.

Kelly got up and started back toward the inn. Either she was totally nuts, and there had been no skeletal hand, or there *had* been a hand, and Nick had somehow done something with it. Neither choice was very appealing. But she began to wonder about him again. Why had he been in the lifeguard office? Why was she so trusting of him?

Kelly went inside and ducked under the ropes around the indoor pool. The indoor pool area was strangely quiet. No one was around, and even the sloshing sounds of the pool were absent. She walked up to the door of the lifeguard office and was about to slide her key into the lock when she heard something creak inside. It sounded as if someone was opening the file cabinet.

Kelly hesitated. No one was supposed to be in there. Only she and Martin had keys.

But Nick had that card . . .

Kelly took a deep breath and slid the key into the lock. She turned the knob and pushed the door open. Nick was standing in front of the open file cabinet. He looked up and stared at her.

"What are you doing in here?" Kelly asked.

Nick didn't seem surprised to see her. "Come in and close the door," he ordered.

Kelly went in, but she left the door open a little bit, just to be safe. Besides, it was hot inside.

"I'm looking for Laura," he said.

"Laura?" Kelly was confused for a moment. Then she remembered. "The bracelet we found this morning?"

"That's right."

"I don't understand," Kelly said.

"Something happened here a long time ago," Nick said. "Something bad. I want to find out what it was."

"How do you know this Laura had anything to do with it?" Kelly asked.

"I don't," Nick said. "But I don't have anything else to go on, so I'm looking into whatever comes up."

"But you don't know what happened?" Kelly asked.

"No."

"So why do you even care?"

"My father was here when it happened," Nick said. "Actually, both of my parents were. Whatever it was, it changed my father forever."

"Oh." Kelly still didn't know what was going on, but at least Nick was starting to confide in her a little bit.

Nick slid the cabinet shut. "Anyway, there's nothing in here about anyone named Laura. It's just another dead end. I'm hot. Let's get out of here."

"Wait," Kelly said.

Nick looked surprised. "What?"

"They didn't find it."

"The skeleton?" Nick guessed.

"Yeah," Kelly said. "I *know* I felt it. I know I wasn't imagining it. The skeleton was there, Nick. Now it isn't there anymore, and you and I are the only ones who knew about it."

Nick gave her an amused look. "I get it. So if we're the only ones who knew about it, and you didn't take it, that means I did."

Suddenly Kelly felt a little embarrassed. When Nick put it that way it sounded a little strange.

"Listen, Kelly," Nick said. "I have no skeletons

hiding in my closet."

"Then where is it?"

"You think because I've been here four days longer than you, I have all the answers?" Nick replied.

"So you're saying it just disappeared?" Kelly asked.

"I'm saying I don't know," Nick said. "It's just another mystery about this place."

Kelly frowned. "Speaking of mysteries, I found a little surprise in my room earlier today."

Kelly told Nick about the note she had found on her pillow. She also told him about Sarah and her necklace.

"I think you're probably right about the note," Nick said. "It sounds like a lame joke to me. As far as that red-haired girl and your necklace, I haven't got a clue." Nick wiped a bead of sweat off of his forehead. "But I have an even bigger mystery."

"What?" Kelly asked.

"Why we're standing in this hot room when we could be outside."

Nick was right; it was hot in the office—too hot. Kelly turned to the door. Then she stopped.

"What's wrong?" Nick asked.

"The door," Kelly said. "It's closed now. I had left it open a bit."

"Well, it doesn't matter," Nick said. "Just open it."

Kelly reached for the doorknob and pulled, but

the door didn't budge. She pushed against the door, but it still wouldn't open. She backed away and felt the blood drain from her face.

"We're locked in," she said.

Chapter 12

"You've got a key," Nick said.

"There's no keyhole on this side," Kelly said. "Maybe you can use your card."

Nick stepped past her and slid the card between the door and the door frame. He pushed and pulled and tried to jimmy it, but the door wouldn't open.

"It won't work," he said. "It's the way the bolt is shaped. I can use the card from the outside, but not from the inside."

"So what do we do?" Kelly asked.

Nick looked around the room. "No windows. One door we can't get through." He shook his head. "You got me."

"We can't just stay in here," Kelly said. "It's too hot. There's no air."

Nick looked back at the door. "Okay, there is one thing we could do. We could try to take the hinge pins out. But we need a hammer and a screwdriver."

They searched the desk. There was no hammer or screwdriver, but they did find a three-hole punch with a flat edge that Nick thought he could use instead of a screwdriver.

Nick opened a button on his shirt and rolled the sleeves up to his elbows. Dark patches of sweat had soaked through the fabric. "It's boiling in here," he said, looking around. "All we need now is something I can use for a hammer."

They searched around and finally found a piece of broken brick that must have been used at times to hold the door open. Nick kneeled in front of the door and held the edge of the three-hole punch against the lower door hinge. Then he banged the brick against the other end of the hole punch.

Clank! The punch slid off the hinge pin. Nick shook his head and wiped his brow with his sleeve. "This isn't going to be easy."

He lined up the hole punch and hit it again, and again.

"Is it working?" Kelly asked. Her stomach was starting to hurt.

"Let's just say I'm making microscopic progress," Nick said.

"You'd think someone could hear us," Kelly said, wiping some sweat off her own forehead.

"The pool's closed," Nick said. "It's almost dinnertime. I doubt anyone's around."

He hit the hole punch again and again. Kelly could see the dark patches of sweat growing on his light-blue shirt. The room felt like a sauna.

"I wonder who closed the door," she said.

Nick looked up at her and wiped more sweat off his brow. His brown hair lay wet and matted on his head. "Why did you leave it open?"

"I wasn't sure about you," Kelly admitted.

Nick looked up at her with a hurt, surprised look on his face. Then he nodded. "Yeah, I can see how you might feel that way. I mean, not that I ever thought of myself as the kind of guy who went around stealing skeletons. But believe me, you have nothing to worry about."

"From you," Kelly said. "But someone closed that door. And locked it."

"Yeah." Nick banged the hinge pin some more.

"You don't seem surprised," Kelly said.

"Nothing that happens here surprises me," Nick said.

Even though her stomach had begun to hurt more, Kelly felt relieved. "So you've noticed that too."

Nick nodded as he worked.

"What do you think is going on?" Kelly asked.

"I don't know," Nick said. "Things are just weird here. Everything goes wrong. Everything seems to work against you." He smacked the brick against the hole punch again. "Like this hinge. I swear, any other hinge pin in the world would have come out by now. This one's barely moved a quarter of an inch."

Kelly watched as Nick kept working on the hinge. By now his blue shirt was completely soaked with sweat. It was growing hotter and more stuffy in the room, as if the body heat Nick was generating from the work was making it worse.

"It's getting hard to breathe," she said.

"I know," Nick said. "This room was never meant to be an office. It was probably just supposed to be an equipment room or something."

Kelly suddenly had a frightening thought. "You don't think we could suffocate, do you?"

Nick hit the hole punch again, and again it slipped off the hinge pin. "Like I said, Kelly, nothing that happens in this place would surprise me."

It took forever, but Nick finally got the bottom hinge pin out.

"One down, one to go." He staggered to his feet and stared at the upper hinge.

"Maybe you ought to take a rest," Kelly said.

"I want to get out of here tonight," Nick said. "Alive."

He was right. The air had become so stale and stuffy that Kelly constantly felt out of breath no matter how hard she breathed. Her body was completely sapped of energy. She could barely think straight.

Nick dragged the chair over to the door and

stood on it. He started to work on the upper hinge the same way he had on the lower one. Kelly was starting to feel dizzy; her head was spinning. She had to sit on the floor with her back against the desk. As she watched Nick bang away at the upper hinge pin, she worried that he might pass out from the exertion and lack of fresh air.

Miraculously, the upper hinge pin came out faster than the lower pin had. A few moments later, Nick managed to work the door off the hinges. A wave of cool, fresh air swept into the room. Kelly took a deep breath and gave a sigh of relief. Exhausted, Nick slumped down beside her, his head bowed between his legs.

Kelly didn't know how long they stayed like that, just sitting and breathing deeply in the fresh air. Through the open doorway, she could see the indoor pool area. The lights were off and it was dark, but she could smell the chlorine in the air and hear the sound of water lapping against the pool's walls.

They must have refilled the pool while they were stuck in the office. Next to her, Nick lifted his head and breathed in deeply. "Ah, the wonderful smell of chlorine."

Suddenly he stood up and began to peel off his sweat-soaked shirt.

"What are you doing?" Kelly asked.

"After spending hours working and sweating in a cramped, hot little room, what do you think I'm

83

doing?" Nick asked as he pulled off his shoes. "I'm going for a swim."

He stepped through the doorway and walked toward the pool. Kelly listened to the sound of the cool water lapping and swirling. It sounded like a good idea. She stood up and started to follow. By now Nick was standing in the dark at the edge of the pool.

Behind him Kelly could just picture the refreshing dark water.

Nick swung his arms back as if he was going to do a racing dive.

Suddenly an odd thought struck Kelly.

How could the pool have been filled so quickly?

It was totally impossible.

Nick crouched down. He was about to spring headfirst into the pool.

"Wait!" Kelly cried.

Chapter 13

Nick turned and faced her in the dim light. "What's wrong?"

"Listen," Kelly said.

Nick listened. "What? I don't hear anything."

"Yeah, I know," Kelly said. "And what did you hear a moment ago?"

"The sounds of the pool water." Nick scowled. "That's weird. I heard it a second ago. Now I don't."

Kelly found a kickboard lying on the floor. She picked it up and tossed it into the pool. Instead of a splash, they heard a dull thud as it hit the pool floor.

"It's empty. There's no water," Nick whispered in amazement. "How did you know?"

"It suddenly occurred to me that there hadn't been time to fill the pool," Kelly said. "It would take all night."

Nick stared back at the pool. "Maybe it was a mirage. Like being in the desert without water and imagining an oasis."

"Except we both heard it," Kelly said.

"We were also both breathing the same bad air," Nick said. "Maybe it played tricks with our minds."

"We both imagined the same exact thing?" Kelly asked skeptically.

"How else would you explain it?" Nick asked as he slipped his shoes back on.

Kelly could only shrug. "I don't know, Nick. I really don't know."

Tired and disturbed by the strange events, they walked through the spa back toward the inn. Kelly looked at her watch. They'd missed dinner. Not that she was hungry now, but she might be later, when her stomach calmed down.

As they started to cross the lobby, the doors to the dining room opened and Eric, Tiffany, and some of the other lifeguards came out.

"Hey, there you are!" Eric said. "We were wondering what happened to you guys."

Tiffany eyed them suspiciously. Kelly realized her hair was damp and disheveled. Nick's hair hung limp on his forehead, and he was bare-chested. He carried his sweat-soaked shirt in his hand.

"Where *have* you two been?" Tiffany asked.

Nick and Kelly glanced at each other.

"We went for a walk and got lost," Nick said.

"Looks like it must have been a long, energetic

walk," Eric said with a raised eyebrow.

Nick shrugged. Feeling Eric's questioning eyes on her, Kelly stared at the ground.

"We were going to the disco," Claire said. "You guys want to meet us there later?"

Again Nick and Kelly glanced at each other.

"I think I'm going to skip it tonight," Nick said. "I'm really bushed."

"So am I," Kelly said. "I'll see you in the morning."

"Sleep well," Tiffany said, staring knives at Kelly.

When the lifeguards gathered for work the next morning, Kelly told them they had the day off again. The previous day the workmen had encountered an unexpected problem and they hadn't been able to refill the pool.

Tiffany glared at Kelly during the brief meeting. Kelly didn't appreciate the other girl's attitude, but she wasn't surprised by it. Tiffany and the other lifeguards left the pool area, but Eric stopped and turned back to Kelly.

"Uh, Kelly?"

"Yes?"

"Uh . . ." For once Eric seemed to be at a loss for words. "Nothing." He shrugged and went out.

Later Kelly was lying on a lounge on the terrace when she heard the scraping of metal against concrete. She looked up to find Nick pulling up a lounge next to hers. She was glad to see him.

"What are your plans for the day?" he asked.

"I don't have any," Kelly replied. "What about you?"

"I have only one thing on the agenda," Nick said with a smile. "And that's spending the day with you."

They spent the morning lying in the sun, then took a picnic lunch down to the waterfront. After they ate, they took a small sailboat out and sailed on the lake. Kelly was growing more comfortable with Nick, even though he was still pretty vague about himself. When she asked what had happened so many years ago with his father, Nick replied that he couldn't talk about it.

Somehow Kelly trusted Nick despite all his mysteries. Whatever he was hiding, she felt that she and Nick were on the same side. She would help him if she could. She sensed that he would do the same for her.

That evening they skipped dinner with the other lifeguards and had a cookout by themselves. And while everyone else went to the disco, she and Nick held hands and walked along the lake.

As the end to a perfect day, they stood in the moonlight and kissed. All of Kelly's worries and concerns seemed a million miles away.

Later Nick walked Kelly to her room on the third floor. Kelly stopped outside the door and turned to him.

"I had a really nice time today," he said, looking into her eyes.

"Me, too."

"I guess tomorrow it's back to work for you."

Kelly nodded. "You'll be around, won't you?"

"Sure," Nick said. "Will I see you again tomorrow night?"

"Definitely." Kelly reached up and kissed him quickly on the lips.

"See you in the morning," Nick said, turning toward the elevator. Suddenly Kelly grabbed his sleeve.

"Wait," she said. Carefully she turned the doorknob and pushed open the door to her room.

"What is it?" Nick asked behind her.

"I just wanted to make sure everything was okay inside."

"Is it?"

"Yes." Kelly smiled at him. "See you in the morning."

She stood in the doorway and watched Nick walk down the hall to the elevator. When the elevator came, they waved to each other one last time. Then Kelly closed the door and wedged the chair against it. She felt happy and warm. It was hard to say good-bye to Nick and she was eager to see him again tomorrow.

She got ready for bed, then turned off the light and walked over to the window. She looked out into the darkness, expecting to see the aqua glow of the underwater lights illuminating the pool. Water had been running into the pool all day, and it should have been filled by now.

Frowning, Kelly pressed her face against the glass, straining to see the pool. *What in the world . . .*

It was glowing, all right.

It was glowing red.

Blood red.

Chapter 14

Kelly slept poorly that night. She tossed and turned and had terrible nightmares, but in the morning she couldn't recall what the dreams were about. The glowing redness of the pool water had disturbed her, but in the end she'd decided it was probably caused by a rusty pipe or some sediment kicked up by the process of refilling the pool.

When she finally got out of bed the next morning, she went to the window and looked down. A light fog hung in the air, and she couldn't see the water clearly. Kelly decided to have an early breakfast and get to the pool before the rest of the lifeguards. The pool had been closed for two days, and she wanted to make sure everything was just right before she reopened it.

But when she got down to the pool, the water was cloudy. Kelly couldn't see the bottom. She went into the office and got the water-testing kit.

Maybe it needed chlorine or some acid to balance the pH levels.

She kneeled by the pool, filled the tester, and added the chemicals. Oddly enough, the test kit showed the chemical levels of the pool water were perfect. Kelly poured it out and retested it, but once again the levels were fine.

Then Kelly remembered the declouder. She went out to the little building and added a cup of the blue crystals to the filtering system. There, that should clear the water up.

But it didn't. As the lifeguard crew gathered for their morning meeting, the pool remained cloudy. Eric was the first to arrive.

"Are we back in business today?" he asked.

"I'm afraid not," Kelly said. "Look at the water."

Eric looked down at the murky liquid. "Oh, wow, man, what's wrong with it?"

"I wish I knew," Kelly said.

For the third morning in a row, Kelly had to tell the lifeguards that the pool would be closed that day. Of course, that meant another day off, and no one was really upset. After they'd left, Kelly went into the office to see if there was any literature on pool-water problems.

She was just putting her key in the lock when it suddenly struck her that the door was back on its hinges! Kelly stepped back and stared at the door. How come it had gotten fixed so quickly and *her* lock was still broken?

Kelly sighed and shook her head. The problem with her door was going on too long. She was going to have to talk to someone other than Sebastian about having it fixed. She let herself into the office and used the piece of brick to keep the door open. Sitting down at the desk, she started to look through the drawers. In one of them she found a handbook on pool maintenance. She was thumbing through it when someone knocked on the door. Kelly turned around and saw Martin standing in the doorway.

"Can I come in?" he asked.

"Sure."

Martin came in and leaned against the desk. "Why is the pool closed?"

"The water's cloudy," Kelly said.

"Did you test it?"

Kelly nodded. "The pH and chlorine levels are fine."

"Did you try the declouder?"

"Yes."

Martin rubbed his chin. "That's funny. That stuff always worked before. What do you think the problem is?"

"I really don't know," Kelly said. "I've been looking through this handbook, but it doesn't mention anything that fits the description."

Martin crossed his arms and frowned. "Well, I'll tell you what I think. I think you ought to open the pool. At least give people the chance to swim if they want."

"But I can't," Kelly said. "If the water's cloudy like that, it'll be hard to see anyone underwater. And who knows what that stuff is, anyway? It could be dangerous."

"Tell you what," Martin said, getting up. "Let's go see just how bad it is."

He went out to the pool, and Kelly followed.

"Now, you go sit up in the lifeguard chair and I'll dive down to the deepest part of the pool," Martin said, pulling off his shirt. "See if you can see me."

Kelly climbed up in the chair, and Martin dove into the pool. His image grew hazier and hazier as he swam toward the bottom. A moment later he swam up and broke through the surface.

"So?" he asked, gasping for breath.

"I could just barely see you," Kelly said.

"But you *could* see me, right?" Martin asked as he swam to the side of the pool.

"Well, yes, but if I didn't know you were there I might have missed you," Kelly said.

Martin pulled himself out of the pool and stood at the edge. "Well, I still think you better open the pool, Kelly."

"Are you serious?" Kelly was shocked. "What if that stuff is poisonous?"

"The water's fine. It felt fine, smells fine, *is* fine." Martin nodded. "A lot of the guests like to

94

swim. They understood when we told them the pool would be closed for one day. They started to complain when we told them it would be closed for two days. If we say it's closed today, people are going to pack up and leave."

"But it's not safe," Kelly said.

"It's safe enough," Martin said, picking up his shirt and shoes and heading for the men's locker room. "Now open it."

Kelly went to the front desk. Sarah was standing behind it as usual. Kelly stared at her neck, but Sarah's blouse was buttoned to the top. Kelly couldn't tell if she was wearing the cross.

"Can I help you?" Sarah asked.

"I'd like to speak to the manager," Kelly said.

"Is something wrong?" Sarah asked.

"Yes."

"Maybe you could tell me," Sarah said.

"I'd really like to speak to the manager," Kelly insisted. Without a word, Sarah turned around and went through a door.

Kelly waited. The most important point she wanted to bring up with the manager was why she felt they shouldn't open the pool. After that she'd discuss the broken lock on her door. And maybe if she was lucky, she'd even get him to open the safe so she could check her jewelry.

It seemed as though Sarah made her wait forever. Finally the red-haired girl returned to the desk. "I'm afraid the manager isn't here," she said.

Kelly stared at her in disbelief. If the manager wasn't there, where had Sarah been for the last fifteen minutes?

"When will he be back?" Kelly asked.

"I don't know," Sarah said.

"I mean, in a hour, or tomorrow, or next week?"

Sarah just shrugged and shook her head.

"Well, is there someone else in charge when the manager isn't here?" Kelly asked.

"Not really," Sarah said.

"What if there's a problem *you* need to talk to the manager about?" Kelly asked.

"I guess I'd just have to wait," Sarah said. Some guests came to the desk. "You'll have to excuse me." She turned and helped the guests.

Kelly left the front desk. How could the manager go away and not leave someone in charge? As she walked back to the pool, it occurred to Kelly that she'd never actually spoken to her boss. She didn't even know who her boss was.

A few minutes later, Kelly opened the pool. She didn't feel she had a choice. Martin wasn't her boss, but he obviously had some authority. Instead of having one lifeguard per pool, she decided to have two at each pool all day. And she would be in the lifeguard chair for that day. As long as the pool was dangerous, she would be personally responsible for the safety of the guests.

She assigned Chip and Tiffany to the outdoor pool while she and Claire watched the indoor pool.

"Just keep a super-close watch on anyone who dives off the board or swims in the deep end," she told Claire, who nodded nervously.

It was just Kelly's luck that several families had arrived the night before with a bunch of eleven- and twelve-year-old boys who were totally wild. As the morning progressed and the kids played around the pool, Kelly couldn't remember ever having to blow her whistle so much.

Breeeet! "No running around the pool!"

Breeeet! "No splashing!"

Breeeet! "No pushing!"

Breeeet! "No cannonballs off the side!"

Breeeet! "No balls in the pool!"

Whenever she whistled them, they'd obey her for five minutes, then start doing something else wrong. Claire was almost no help. Some of the boys were as big as she was, and it seemed to Kelly that Claire was intimidated by them.

As the morning wore on, Kelly was really starting to look forward to her lunch break. She'd have to get Chip or Eric to cover for her and handle the kids, but at least she'd have an hour to go off and relax. She hoped she'd be able to find Nick. She was dying to see him.

"Hey, where's Joey?" a voice shouted.

Kelly looked up and blinked. The wild kids were standing by the edge of the pool, talking and gesturing.

"I saw him dive into the deep end," said one.

"Me, too, but I didn't see him come up," said another.

Kelly felt a chill and stood up, peering into the cloudy water at the deep end of the pool. Suddenly she saw the hazy outline of a body!

With a burst of adrenaline, Kelly launched herself straight off the chair and into the water. She kicked and stroked with all her might down toward the unmoving figure.

Chapter 15

Kelly had no time to think as she dove toward the inert body lying on the bottom of the pool. She slid her hands under his arms and launched herself upward. Seconds later she reached the edge of the pool. Claire was waiting there to help Kelly pull the limp body out of the water. They placed the boy on his back beside the pool.

"Start CPR!" Kelly shouted at Claire as she pulled herself out of the pool.

Claire leaned on her knees over the boy and tilted his head back, then hesitated uncertainly. To Kelly she was moving much too slowly. Valuable seconds were being lost . . .

"I'll do it!" Kelly snapped and replaced Claire beside the boy. She grabbed his wet head and reached to open his mouth.

Splat! A mouthful of pool water splashed into her face. Kelly straightened up, stunned. She wiped the water out of her eyes and looked down. The boy was grinning at her! Suddenly she heard laughter. The boy's friends were standing around her, laughing.

The boy she'd just "saved" jumped to his feet and pointed his finger at her.

"Fooled you!" he shouted and laughed. "Fooled you!"

Kelly felt weak. She'd been convinced that the boy was drowning . . . and all along it was just a joke. She could feel tears welling up in her eyes. Trembling, she stood up and walked to the life-guard office. She unlocked the door, went in, and slammed the door behind her.

Kelly sat down at the desk and sobbed.

After a while someone knocked on the door. Kelly raised her head and wiped the tears out of her eyes. "Who is it?"

"Claire. Is there anything I can do?"

"Get Eric and tell him to watch the pool," Kelly said. "Then find Martin and tell him what happened."

Kelly soon stopped crying, but she didn't leave the office. She felt overwhelmed and worn out by the constant feeling of uncertainty in the air, the sense that things were never quite right at the New Arcadia. It seemed as if no one was in charge, and nothing worked the way it should. All her life, Kelly had stuck with difficult tasks and challenges, and triumphed. She'd never been a quitter. But now Kelly was starting to wonder. What was the point? What was she going through all this anxiety for?

There was another knock on the door.

"Who is it?" Kelly asked.

"Nick. Can I come in?"

Kelly blinked and quickly looked around for a mirror. She knew she must look like a mess. There was no mirror or anything else she could see herself in. She stood up and opened the door. Nick stared in at her.

"I heard what happened," he said. "Are you okay?"

Kelly pushed the door shut behind him. Nick put his arms around her and hugged her closely.

"I don't know," she said.

"I heard Martin is going to talk to the kids' parents," Nick said. "If anything like that happens again, those kids'll be banned from the pool."

Kelly nodded. "It's not just that, Nick. This whole place gives me the creeps. I mean, I'm really starting to wonder what I'm doing here."

"I know how you feel," Nick said.

Kelly had an idea, and looked up at him. "Maybe we could both go somewhere else."

Nick smiled down at her and hugged her. "I can't, Kelly. I have to stay here."

"Why?"

"Because I do."

"I wish you'd tell me what this is all about," Kelly said.

"Believe me," Nick said. "I would if I could."

Chapter 16

Over the next week, things quieted down at the New Arcadia. There were no weird incidents, and no accidents at the pool. The rowdy kids and their parents left, and Kelly began to relax at her job. She still couldn't get the pool water completely clear, but she tried not to let it bother her. The murky water wasn't hurting anyone, so Kelly figured she might as well let it be.

Kelly and Nick spent more and more time together. They even started eating dinner together at a table separate from the lifeguard crew. One night while they were eating alone, Kelly suddenly felt someone standing over them. She looked up and saw Tiffany.

"I hardly ever see you two anymore," Tiffany said, staring right at Nick.

Kelly and Nick glanced at each other.

"I guess you must have really important things

to talk about," Tiffany said, now turning to Kelly. "Or maybe you feel you're too good to sit with the rest of us."

Kelly didn't know what to say. She just stared down at the table.

"That's really not necessary, Tiffany," Nick said.

Tiffany shrugged and walked away.

"Don't let it get to you," Nick told Kelly. "She's just jealous."

"I know," Kelly said. "I just don't know why she has to act so mean."

"It's not important," Nick said.

A group of older people sat down at the next table. Kelly hadn't seen any of them before, so they must have just arrived that day. They looked like they were in their forties and fifties. They began talking loudly, and Nick and Kelly couldn't help overhearing.

"Looks like they did a pretty good job renovating this place."

"Yeah, it's hard to imagine it's the same inn we used to come to in the sixties."

Kelly noticed that Nick suddenly tensed.

"Used to be pretty wild around here," someone at the other table said.

"You're not kidding. A lot of strange stuff happened."

"Well, that's what we used to hear, anyway."

"Steve's right. I never saw any of it myself."

"But remember that triple murder? That crazy jealous girl? That one was in all the papers."

"Well, sure, but that was the early seventies," someone said. "By then all the hippies had taken over and the place was just a big commune. They closed it down after that. But a lot of strange stuff went on even before that. I mean, back when it was still being run as an inn."

"Oh, yeah, wasn't there a story about some kid whose parents beat him?"

"There was that one. And the one about the girl who drowned and they hid the body."

Nick sat perfectly still. It seemed to Kelly that the blood was draining out of his face.

"I never heard that story."

"Well, it seemed there was a party one night. Some kids and lifeguards. Anyway, they were drinking and things got kind of out of hand. The next thing they knew, this girl was lying on the bottom of the pool. They tried to revive her, but she must've been on the bottom for a while, because she was stone cold."

"Sounds like it was an accident. I mean, not that they should have been drinking, but it wasn't like anyone intentionally meant to harm her."

"Well, that's where the story gets interesting. You see, what I heard was that instead of reporting it to the authorities, the others just decided to get rid of the body."

"You think maybe there was foul play?"

"I can't say. All I heard was that the body disappeared and was never seen again."

Kelly was watching Nick. He'd turned white as a ghost. She reached over and shook his arm gently. "Nick?"

He didn't react. Kelly wasn't even sure he'd heard her.

"Nick?" she said again.

He started to slide his chair back.

"Where are you going?" Kelly asked.

Nick didn't answer. He stood up and hurried out of the dining room. Kelly got up and ran after him, but Nick had already rushed through the lobby and out into the night. Kelly lost sight of him in the dark.

"Nick?" she called, walking out into the humid air. It was a warm evening, and thin clouds blocked the stars and moon. Nick could have been anywhere, and she certainly wasn't going into the woods. Not knowing where else to look, she walked around the side of the inn and headed toward the pool. In the distance she could see a lone figure standing on the terrace with his back toward her.

Kelly jogged toward him, then stopped a dozen feet away. "Nick?" she said softly.

The person turned.

Chapter 17

"Martin!" Kelly gasped.

"What are you doing out here?" Martin asked.

"What are *you* doing out here?" Kelly asked back.

Martin pointed at the pool. "I was looking at the water."

Kelly stared down at the pool. The underwater pool lights were on, and she could see that the water was still cloudy. "I've done everything I can to get it clear," she said. "I even had the pool company come, but they couldn't clear it either."

Martin nodded slowly. "Maybe it just doesn't *want* to get clear."

Kelly stared at him, puzzled. "I don't think it matters what the water wants. Do you?"

Martin shrugged, continuing to gaze into the murky pool. He was acting weird, but Kelly had other things on her mind.

"Did you see Nick?" she asked.

"Who?"

"A tall, good-looking guy about my age."

"I saw someone go that way." Martin pointed to the trail that led down toward the lakefront.

Kelly turned toward the trail, but then stopped. "Can I ask you a question?"

"Okay."

"Who's my boss?" Kelly asked.

"You don't really have one," Martin said.

"Martin, someone has to be my boss," Kelly said. "I mean, someone has to be in charge."

"Do they?" Martin asked.

Kelly couldn't believe what Martin was saying.

"Look," Martin explained. "You're in charge of the pool. That's all you have to know."

"If I'm in charge of the pool, how come you made me open it when I didn't want to?" Kelly asked.

"Because I knew it had to be opened," Martin replied simply.

Kelly could sense that she wasn't going to get anywhere with this. Like everything else in this place, Martin made no sense.

She turned and headed down the trail toward the lake. A few moments later she came out on the rise above the waterfront. Below on the dock she could see the silhouette of a person staring down at the calm water. Kelly went down the stairs and walked out on the dock. When she was about twenty-five feet away, Nick heard her and looked up.

"Go away," he ordered.

"Why?" Kelly asked.

"Because I don't want to be with anyone."

"Not even me?" Kelly asked.

Nick sighed, his eyes remaining on the water. The moon had broken through the clouds, and a long, sparkling streak of light shimmered across the lake's surface.

"I'm sorry, Kelly," Nick said softly. "Of course I want to be with you."

Kelly came closer and sat down beside him. "What's wrong, Nick?"

"Don't ask."

"It has something to do with that story about the girl who drowned, doesn't it?"

Somewhere in the dark there was a splash, as if a fish had jumped.

"Why can't you tell me?" Kelly asked.

"There's nothing to tell," Nick said. "You know as much as I do."

"No," Kelly said. "That story obviously upset you. To me it was just another weird story about this place. I feel like I've heard so many that it doesn't even matter anymore."

Nick pushed himself to his feet and offered his hand. "Come on, I'll walk you back."

Kelly was disappointed. "You still won't tell me?"

Nick shook his head.

"Can't we at least hang out together?" Kelly asked.

"Tomorrow," Nick said. "Tonight I have to be by myself."

Kelly let him help her up, and they walked quietly back to the inn. Nick got out on the second floor. He kissed her quickly on the cheek.

"See you in the morning," he said, and walked away.

Kelly rode up to the third floor, wishing she understood what was going on. As she stepped out of the elevator, she saw that someone had stuck a note to the outside of her door. She hurried down the hall and pulled the note off. It said *Dear Kelly, I took a few dives off the board on the outdoor pool today. It felt strange. Maybe you should check it out.* It was signed *Tiffany* in fancy script writing.

That's odd, Kelly thought. She'd just seen Tiffany a little while ago, and the girl had said nothing about the diving board. On the other hand, knowing Tiffany, maybe it wasn't so weird.

First thing the next morning Kelly hurried down to the pool. If there was something wrong with the diving board, it would have to be repaired before the pool opened, or the diving board would have to be off-limits for the day.

The air was still a bit chilly that early in the morning. Kelly stuck her toe in the water. It felt warm. She walked over to the diving board and inspected it. Nothing looked wrong. She climbed the metal steps and stepped up onto the board. The surface felt wet from the morning dew. Kelly walked out to the end. The board bent and creaked slightly. She bounced gently up on her toes and felt the spring of the board. It felt okay to her.

She bent her knees and bounced again, this time springing higher into the air. The board bent, but felt firm when she landed. On the next bounce she sprang even higher. As she came down, her feet hit the board again.

Crack! The board snapped like a twig.

Splash!

Kelly hit the water face first.

Chapter 18

Kelly could hear laughter.

Terrible, taunting laughter . . .

It was the laughter of a young woman.

Kelly opened her eyes. Everything was a blue blur. Her eyes stung. She was floating underwater. Suddenly the realization of what had happened hit her. The board had snapped. She'd hit the water and was stunned.

Ah ha ha ha haaaaa!

Why was she still hearing the laughter? Was this a dream? No, her lungs screamed for air. Surrounded by water and hideous laughter, Kelly swam desperately toward the surface.

"Ahh!" She broke though the surface and gasped for air, then coughed violently. She'd inhaled some water. She reached the side of the pool and clung to it, racked with spasms of coughing.

Tiffany, she thought.

When she'd regained her breath, Kelly pulled herself out of the pool. Grabbing a towel, she wrapped it around her shoulders, marched into the inn, and took the elevator up to the third floor. Still dripping pool water, she stood outside Tiffany's room and knocked.

"Who is it?" Tiffany called from inside.

"Kelly."

A second later the door swung open. Tiffany had a puzzled look on her face, but Kelly had expected that.

"It wasn't funny," Kelly said.

"What?"

"Sabotaging the diving board," Kelly said. "Don't pretend you don't know what I'm talking about."

"I don't."

Kelly rolled her eyes. "Come on, Tiffany. You left me a note saying to check out the diving board."

"Where?"

"On my door." Kelly pointed down the hall. Tiffany stepped out into the hall and looked.

"I don't see a note," she said.

"Of course you don't," Kelly snapped. "You left it last night. I took it inside. The only thing I can't figure out is how you got that laughter underwater."

Tiffany turned and stared at Kelly. "Laughter

114

underwater? I think you've gone psycho, Kelly."

Kelly glared at her. She could prove it. It was simple. She marched down the hall to her room, pushed open the door, and went in. She'd left the note on the desk. She'd simply take it back to Tiffany and stick it in her face.

But her desk was bare. Kelly looked on the floor, then around the bed, then in the bathroom. The note was gone. Suddenly Kelly understood. She left her room, stormed down to Tiffany's door, and knocked again.

Tiffany pulled open the door. "Now what?"

"You went into my room and took the note back," Kelly said.

Tiffany rolled her eyes. "How could I do that?"

"Easy," Kelly said, just barely able to contain her rage. "You pushed open the door, took the note off the desk, and left."

"Right." Tiffany smirked. "Like I have a key to your room."

"You don't need a key," Kelly said. "The lock on my door is broken."

"Oh?" Tiffany's eyebrows went up.

A shadow of a doubt began to creep into Kelly's mind. Either Tiffany was telling the truth or she was an excellent actress.

"So I sabotaged the diving board and then left you a note and then made laughter underwater and then stole the note from your room," Tiffany said. "So, are you mad because I sabotaged the diving board or took the note?"

"I'm mad because you asked me . . ." Kelly shook her head. It was all getting too crazy.

"Asked you what?"

Kelly sighed. "Forget it."

"Forget this?" Tiffany smiled. "You're not serious. This is the least forgettable thing that's happened to me since I got here. I'll probably remember this for as long as I live!"

Kelly turned and went back down the hall. She had to tell Martin the diving board was broken.

And that she was quitting.

She was crossing the lobby when she saw Nick coming toward her.

"Hey, Kelly." They stopped in the middle of the lobby and gazed into each other's eyes. Nick bowed his head a little. "Look, I'm sorry about last night."

Kelly nodded silently.

"I guess I was a little rude," Nick said.

"That's okay," Kelly said. "In a few minutes it won't matter."

"What?" Nick looked puzzled. "Why?"

"Because I'm quitting," Kelly said. "Then I'm leaving."

Nick stared at her with surprised eyes. "Look, if it has anything to do with me, I just told you I was sorry."

"It's something else," Kelly admitted.

"Well, what?" Nick asked.

Kelly glanced around. She felt a little uncomfortable standing in the middle of the lobby.

"Let's go sit down," she said, gesturing to a couch near the fireplace.

They walked over to the couch and sat down. Kelly told Nick the whole story of the note and the broken diving board.

"But you can't just quit," Nick said when she'd finished.

"Why not?"

"Who'll be in charge of the lifeguards?"

"At this point, I really don't care," Kelly replied.

"Look, Kelly," Nick said. "If you leave, you're not only leaving the guests in danger, you're leaving the other lifeguards in danger too. They need someone to tell them what to do. Without you, everything would be totally disorganized."

Kelly stared at him. "Since when did you become a spokesman for the guests and other lifeguards?"

"I'm just telling it like it is," Nick said. "I know this place is all screwed up and nobody knows who's in charge. That's why you just have to decide you are. I mean, do you really think Eric or Tiffany could be in charge here?"

Kelly shook her head. "I just want to get away

from this place. I've had more than enough of the New Arcadia Inn."

Nick put his hand on her knee. "Listen, Kelly. I know you must be upset about the note and diving board." He paused for a second. "But my guess is what's really bothering you is that Tiffany's going to tell everyone this crazy story. I mean, I know it must be embarrassing."

Kelly sighed and stared at some old, half-burned logs in the fireplace. The note and diving board did bother her. The laughter underwater *really* bothered her. But deep in her heart she knew there had to be an explanation for those things. Nick was right, the thing that *really, really* upset her was knowing that at that very minute Tiffany was probably telling everyone how Kelly had accused her of the whole thing.

"Are you worried that the other lifeguards will all laugh at you?" Nick asked.

Kelly nodded. The thought made her feel like running away.

Nick put his arm around her shoulder. "Here's the deal. We're going to get up and go into the dining room and have breakfast with the other lifeguards."

Kelly turned and stared at him with dread. "Never."

"Yes," Nick said. "You've got to do it. You've got to go in there and face them."

"But they'll laugh at me," Kelly argued.

"Probably," Nick agreed. "And you know what you'll do? You'll laugh along with them. Like you can't believe it either. Like you just can't imagine what got into you this morning."

Kelly stared at him. "Why would I do that?"

"Because if you admit it and laugh at it, then it's no big deal," Nick said. "By this afternoon, they'll pretty much have forgotten about it."

Kelly looked down at the floor. "Maybe you're right, Nick. But I really want to just pack my bags and get out of here."

"Don't, Kelly," Nick urged softly. "I really don't want you to go."

She looked up, and their eyes met. She could feel herself weakening. She wanted to be with him, and she knew he wanted to be with her.

"Give it a try at least," Nick said. "If I'm wrong, then you can decide what to do."

Kelly felt him slide his hand over hers and start to pull her up.

A few minutes later they entered the dining room. Nick held her hand tightly. The lifeguards were all sitting at their table, talking. As Kelly walked toward them, she saw Tiffany glance up at her. For a moment Tiffany looked stunned, then she quickly turned to the others and whispered something. Everyone suddenly quieted and stared at Kelly. She felt as though she wanted to crawl into a cave somewhere and die.

Then she felt Nick squeeze her hand.

Kelly forced a smile onto her face and sat down at the table. The tension around the table felt so thick you could cut it with a knife.

"Hey, guys," Kelly said with a grin. "What's up?"

Tiffany stared at her for a second, then rolled her eyes. Chip looked up at Kelly.

"Tiffany was telling us that the outdoor diving board broke when you jumped on it this morning," he said.

Kelly nodded. "It just snapped."

"Did you really hear laughing?" Claire asked.

Kelly smiled and shook her head wondrously. "Well, I thought I did. But maybe I just hit my head really hard when I hit the water. I mean, has anyone ever heard laughter underwater?"

The lifeguards glanced at one another. Kelly could feel the tension around the table start to disappear.

"Tiffany said you thought she sabotaged the diving board," Eric said.

"I was just really upset," Kelly said with a shrug. "Everyone has a weird day every once in a while."

A few of the other lifeguards nodded. Kelly could see that Tiffany was starting to frown.

"What about the note you said I left on your door and then stole from your room?" she asked.

"Well, there was definitely a note on my door last night and it was signed with your name,"

Kelly said. "All I know is that now the note's gone."

"You know," Chip said, "I've noticed some strange things about this place too. Like in my room the hot and cold water is reversed. And there's a window in my closet."

The next thing Kelly knew, everyone was talking about the strange things they'd noticed about the inn. Most of them didn't sound particularly strange to her, at least not nearly as strange as the things she'd experienced. But at least the others seemed to have forgotten the story about her. She glanced over at Nick and smiled.

Nick winked back.

Chapter 19

Things seemed "normal" for the rest of the day. Both pools were crowded, and Kelly had little time to reflect on the incident with the diving board. By the time the pools closed that evening, it was almost a distant memory.

That night Nick suggested to Kelly that instead of going off by themselves, they should join the lifeguards for dinner. Kelly agreed, and they sat with everyone else around the big table. As dinner was ending, Eric suddenly got an idea.

"Hey, let's have a pool party!" he said.

"How?" Tiffany asked.

"Well, Kelly's in charge of the pool," Eric said. "She could officially declare it open for lifeguards only tonight."

"Can you do that?" Chip asked.

"Well, I guess I could," Kelly replied a little nervously. "I'm not so sure it's a good idea."

"Why?" Tiffany asked. "Afraid the diving board might break?"

Rather than get back on *that* subject, Kelly quickly agreed to the party. After all, Martin had told her she was in charge of the pool.

A little while later they all met at the indoor pool. Eric had even made a sign that said "Pool Closed For Private Party" and taped it to the door. For the first half hour, everyone swam and fooled around in the water. Tiffany, of course, had to show off her dives, especially her double flip.

"Aw, come on," Eric teased her. "Everyone knows you can do that with your eyes closed. Quit showing off."

"You're just jealous," Tiffany replied smugly.

"Am not," Eric snapped back.

"Are too," Tiffany taunted.

"Okay, wait a minute," Nick said. "Instead of arguing, I have a better idea. Why don't we give Eric a chance to show off?"

Eric stared at him uncertainly.

"I'm serious," Nick said. "Now it's your turn to do something impressive."

"Like a hundred push-ups?" Eric asked.

"Aw, we know you can do that," Chip said. "How about something a little more original?"

Eric scratched his head and looked around. "I don't know," he said. "This is kind of dumb. Let's see one of you guys do something."

The lifeguards looked around at one another.

"Hey," Chip said. "I've got something. Let's have a bet. Who wants to bet I can't stay on the bottom of the pool for a whole minute?"

Kelly glanced at the others.

"How will we know if you're really on the bottom?" Eric asked.

"Uh . . . I know," Chip said. "It doesn't get really cloudy until you're at the bottom. So if you can't see me, you'll know I must be down there."

"Sounds okay to me," Eric said. The others nodded. Before long, Chip had taken several bets. He stood by the edge of the pool, taking deep breaths and letting them out slowly.

"Okay, guys, get your money out," Chip said, "because I won't be up again for a minute."

He dove into the pool, swam down to the cloudy part, and disappeared from sight.

Kelly stared down at her watch as the second hand slowly swept around its face. Suddenly she felt uneasy. She just didn't like the idea of someone being down at the bottom of the pool where they couldn't be seen.

The seconds ticked past. *Thirty . . . thirty-five . . . forty . . . forty-five . . .*

"I can't believe he's really going do it," Claire said.

"He hasn't done it yet," Eric replied.

Kelly stared at her watch. *Fifty . . . fifty-five . . . sixty . . .*

"He did it," she said. "He should come up now."

"Maybe he's staying down longer, just to make sure," Eric said. "I mean, it's not like he has an underwater watch or anything."

Kelly kept her eye on her watch. *One minute five, one minute ten, one minute fifteen* . . . Chip was taking too long. Maybe he was okay, but maybe he wasn't.

"I don't like this," she said, and dove into the water.

It didn't take her long to find Chip. She could just barely see him in the cloudy water, but she reached down to touch him. Suddenly he grabbed her wrist and wouldn't let go.

Kelly tried to pull her hand free, but Chip's grip was unshakable. She grabbed his hand and tried to pry his fingers off her wrist, but it was no use. With Chip holding her wrist so tightly, she had only one free hand. Kelly pulled as hard as she could, but Chip's grip on her wrist was like a vise.

Suddenly, Kelly was panic-stricken. If she didn't break loose from Chip soon, they'd both drown!

Chapter 20

Kelly didn't know how long they kept struggling. But suddenly Chip let go and shot toward the surface past her. Kelly raced up behind him. By the time she got to the surface, Chip was holding on to the edge of the pool, gasping loudly for breath.

"Wow, you were down there for almost two minutes!" Eric was telling him as he kneeled at the edge of the pool.

Chip was so busy gasping for breath that he couldn't respond.

"What happened down there?" Nick asked Kelly as he helped her out of the pool.

Kelly just shook her head. "Let Chip tell you."

It took a long time before Chip seemed able to talk. Before he did, he quickly climbed out of the pool and sat on the side, panting and shivering.

"What happened?" Claire asked.

Chip stared up at them with wide, terrified eyes. "I don't know. I mean, I swam down to the bottom where the drain is, you know? But then, when I tried to swim up, suddenly there was a current of water sucking me down. Like there was all this water rushing into the drain and I couldn't fight through it."

His eyes met Kelly's. "Did you feel it, Kelly?"

Kelly shook her head. She didn't remember feeling anything like that. "I tried to pull you up," she said, "but you wouldn't come. It felt like you must have been holding on to something."

"The only thing I was holding on to was you," Chip said, trembling. "I'm really sorry if I scared you, Kelly. But I was scared out of my wits."

"It's okay," Kelly said. "It must have been really frightening."

"I think we ought to have someone take a look at that drain," Chip said. "Someone could get caught down there and drown."

The others nodded pensively. Fortunately Chip was okay, and they started to party again. Like all the other strange things that had happened at the inn, it had been weird and creepy, but no one had been seriously hurt. Pretty soon everyone was laughing and fooling around again. A water fight broke out in the shallow end of the pool, and everyone went running for something that would hold water. Someone came back with several of the white plastic buckets they used to carry chemicals in. People began filling them with water and splashing each other.

Kelly was just climbing out of the pool when she saw Chip pass her with one of the white buckets, sneaking up behind Eric. Chip tapped him on the shoulder, and when Eric turned, Chip heaved the bucket of water into his face. Water splashed everywhere, and Eric sputtered and wiped his eyes.

"Why, you—!" He laughed and shouted, grabbing another white bucket and chasing Chip. Chip got trapped in a corner, and Eric went toward him, holding the bucket back as if preparing to heave it at him.

"No! No! Don't do it, Eric!" Chip cowered in mock fear.

A second later Eric splashed the contents of the bucket into Chip's face.

"*Aaaaaahhhhhh!*" A bloodcurdling scream split the air. Chip fell to his knees and was clutching his eyes as he screamed in agony.

Kelly and the others ran toward him. The smell of chlorine stung her nostrils.

"*My eyes!*" Chip screamed. "They're burning!"

"Get him into the locker room!" Kelly quickly ordered. "Run cold water into his eyes!"

While Eric and Nick carried Chip into the

locker room, Kelly unlocked the lifeguard office and called for an ambulance.

Half an hour later, two emergency medical services technicians helped Chip into the back of their ambulance. Thick wads of gauze covered Chip's eyes. As the ambulance sped off into the dark, Martin asked to speak to the rest of the lifeguards back at the pool.

At the pool, Kelly walked over to the bucket Eric had heaved at Chip. As she looked into it, the liquid chlorine vapors were so strong they made her eyes water.

"Now, can someone tell me what happened?" Martin asked.

"We were all fooling around, having a water fight," Kelly explained. "Someone went out and came back with a couple of the white buckets."

"Who?" Martin asked.

Everyone looked at each other for a moment.

"It was Chip," Claire said. "I saw him go out and come back in with two white buckets."

"It just doesn't make any sense," Eric said. "I saw those two buckets get filled with pool water half a dozen times."

"Did you say *two* buckets?" Nick asked.

"Yeah." Eric nodded.

Nick pointed around the pool area. There was a bucket lying on its side near the pool, another floating upside down in the pool, and then the third bucket—the one that smelled of chlorine.

"There are three buckets!" Kelly gasped.

"But I swear I saw Chip carry in only two," Claire said.

"He could have been carrying one inside the other," Nick said.

"But even if he was, he wouldn't have carried in a bucket filled with liquid chlorine," Kelly said.

"Oh, man." Eric shook his head sadly. "I feel terrible. I mean, what if he's blind?"

"It's not your fault," Kelly said, putting her arm around his shoulder. "No one knew what was in that bucket."

"No one even knows where that bucket came from," Nick reminded him.

"All right," Martin said. "I don't think anyone's at fault here. You'll just have to be more careful. Let's not have any more pool parties."

Martin left the pool area. Soon after that, Tiffany and Claire said they were going back to their room. Eric stayed behind, looking miserable.

"Man, if Chip's eyes are permanently damaged, I'll never forgive myself," he said sadly.

Nick patted him on the back. "I don't think you have to worry. The EMS guys didn't think it was permanent. Don't forget, we swim in a diluted mixture of that stuff every day."

Eric nodded and said he was going to go to the front desk and call the hospital to see what was going on with Chip. That left Nick and Kelly alone at the pool.

"It's like a never-ending series of accidents here," Kelly said.

Nick nodded gravely. "I think we better be more careful, or someone could get really hurt, or—"

"Even die," Kelly finished for him.

Chapter 21

Over the next few days Kelly spoke to Chip on the phone several times. The doctors said his eyes were going to be fine, but they didn't want him to swim again that summer. He wouldn't be able to continue as a lifeguard—he was going home right from the hospital.

The news that Chip was okay was a big relief to the lifeguards, and soon things were almost back to normal. A lifeguard named David was hired to replace Chip. David was handsome, with wavy blond hair and a muscular build that was even better than Eric's. In fact, Eric got depressed as soon as he met David. Meanwhile, Kelly saw immediately that David had replaced Nick as the object of Tiffany's romantic interest.

"Looks like you're off the hook," Kelly whispered to Nick one afternoon as they sat by the pool. Kelly was on duty, and Nick was keeping her company. On the other side of the pool Tiffany was practicing her diving. David sat at the pool's edge with his feet in the water, watching.

"I keep telling you I never was *on* the hook," Nick whispered back.

"Oh, come on," Kelly teased. "You know she liked you."

"Well, it's a good thing she found David," Nick said. "Because I didn't come here to meet anyone."

"You didn't?" Kelly asked.

"Not till I met you," Nick said with a smile.

Across the pool, Tiffany did another dive.

"I wonder when she's going to do her famous double flip?" Kelly asked.

"It's her best dive," Nick said. "Maybe she's saving it for last."

They watched Tiffany rise to the surface, then swim to the side of the pool and climb out. She swept the wet hair out of her eyes and smiled at David.

"Here it comes," Kelly said.

Tiffany climbed up onto the board and walked out to the end. She bounced up and down on her toes, testing the board's spring. Then she walked back to the middle of the board and stood very still.

"Look at how hard she's pretending to concentrate!" Kelly observed. "You'd think it was the first time in her life she'd even tried the dive!"

Nick chuckled.

Tiffany took two long strides and then sprang up into the air from the end of the diving board. She began to curl gracefully into the first part of the dive, but suddenly, at the top of her arc, her body twisted unnaturally. A second later she splashed into the water face first in a way that snapped her head back.

Intuitively sensing that something was wrong, Kelly sprang to her feet. On the other side of the pool, David stared at the water for a moment, then dove in. Kelly raced around the side of the pool and reached Tiffany just as David brought her to the surface. Kelly could instantly see that something was really wrong. Tiffany's neck was bent in an unusual way, and her eyes were glassy.

"It's her neck!" David shouted.

Kelly spun around and waved at Nick. "Bring the body splint!" she shouted. "And tell someone to call an ambulance."

She splashed into the water. "Don't try to lift her out!" she told David. "We'll get her on the body splint and stabilize her head and neck."

Everything happened so fast. Kelly and David held Tiffany in the water so that she could breathe. Tiffany's eyes were open, but they were unfocused. Kelly was almost certain the girl was in shock. Nick jumped in the water with the body splint, and they got it under her and strapped her body to it.

135

"Towels and blankets!" Kelly shouted.

Nick quickly climbed out of the pool. Kelly turned to David.

"Is she secure on the splint?" she asked.

"I think so," David said.

"Okay, let's lift her carefully out of the water," Kelly instructed. She tried to take a step, but something was caught around her ankle. Kelly was too involved with saving Tiffany to think about it. She tried to kick free, and when the thing holding her foot wouldn't let go, she kicked even harder.

Her foot came free. Kelly thought she heard something like laughter and then the words "too bad, too bad . . ." but in all the splashing and yelling, she couldn't be sure.

She and David carried Tiffany to the side of the pool. Nick came back, and they swaddled Tiffany in towels and blankets. It wasn't long before the ambulance came.

Kelly felt Nick put his arm around her shoulders as they watched the grim sight of the EMS attendants wheeling Tiffany away on a stretcher. Then Kelly pressed her face into Nick's chest and began to sob. Something was terribly wrong at the New Arcadia.

It was almost as if the resort was cursed.

Chapter 22

That evening the lifeguards sat in numb silence in the dining room. A few of them had gone up to the buffet for food, but now their plates sat untouched on the table.

"I just don't get it," Eric said. "I mean, first Chip, now Tiffany."

Claire hugged herself and shivered. "It makes you wonder who's next."

Kelly had been thinking the same thing. Then she noticed Nick glance at her and nod. He seemed to be reminding her that she was in charge.

"I know it's tempting to think that one of us has to be next," Kelly said. "But I really think it's just two unfortunate accidents in a row."

"It's hard to believe they were accidents," Eric said. "I mean, what was that bucket filled with liquid chlorine doing by the side of the pool? And how many times did Tiffany do that dive perfectly? Personally, I think this place is whacked. I mean, the weirdest things keep happening here."

Kelly wanted to tell him that he didn't know half of the story, but she knew if she did the rest of her lifeguards just might quit. Of course, Kelly wasn't sure she could blame them if they did.

No one wanted to go to the disco that night. Kelly went up to her room. She was standing at the window, staring down at the pool, when she heard a knock.

"Who is it?" she asked.

"Nick."

"Come in."

Nick pushed the door open. "I see your door still hasn't been fixed."

Kelly shrugged. "I've given up on it. I haven't even seen Sebastian for the last few days, and I don't know who else to ask."

Nick nodded and sat down on the bed. "After a while you start to wonder whether this place is a resort or a funny farm. There's just so much bizarre stuff going on."

Kelly sat down on the bed beside him. "You want to hear some more?"

Nick shrugged. "It's gonna have to be pretty impressive after what happened today."

"This afternoon, while I was in the pool helping David rescue Tiffany, I felt something grab hold of my ankle again."

138

"You sure?" Nick asked.

Kelly nodded. "I felt it grab and hold, but I was so pumped up that I was able to kick free. The other thing is, I think I heard someone laugh and say, 'too bad.'"

Nick stared at her. "So now the pool talks too?"

Kelly nodded. "I guess so."

"Wow, the creature from the bottom of the pool," Nick said. "Was that on TV once?"

"It's not funny, Nick," Kelly said. "I really don't see how I can let anyone in that pool tomorrow. I don't even want to go in it myself."

Nick slid his arm across her shoulder. "I hate to say it, but I don't blame you."

Kelly looked into his eyes. "Why can't we leave, Nick? I would if you would."

Nick didn't answer. Kelly felt him take a deep breath and sigh. Then he stood up, walked to the window, and looked out toward the pool.

"My father committed suicide last year," Nick said. His words hung in the air. Kelly didn't know what to say. Nick reached into his pocket and took out a white envelope with a rubber band around it. He pulled off the rubber band, opened the envelope, and took out some photographs.

"These are pictures of my mother and father," he said, handing the photos to Kelly.

She took the photos and looked at them. They must have been taken in the sixties. Nick's father had sideburns, and his mother was wearing green bell-bottom pants. Kelly could see the family resemblance. Nick looked very much like his father, but he had his mother's eyes.

"They used to come here a lot," Nick said. "Then something happened and they never came back."

"You think what happened here had something to do with why your father killed himself?" Kelly asked.

"Yes."

"How do you know?"

"My father's friends told me," Nick said. "After what happened here, my father changed. It was like, before that he was a great, happy guy, and after that he began a long, slow decline. He went to college and became a history professor. But he couldn't hold a job. The last four years, he was in and out of mental institutions. Finally he convinced them he was better just long enough for them to let him out. Then he killed himself."

His words shook Kelly. As she looked through the photographs, she noticed that in several of them Nick's parents were joined by a handsome young man and a young woman with long, straight blond hair parted in the middle.

"Do you know who they are?" Kelly asked, pointing at them.

Nick shook his head. "I think they must have

been friends of my parents. But I don't know who."

"Did you ever ask your mother?" Kelly asked.

Nick shook his head and looked back down at the pool.

"Nick?"

"I didn't get these pictures until after my father died," he said. "They were in the pocket of the jacket he was wearing when he killed himself."

"I still don't understand why you didn't ask your mother what happened," Kelly said.

Nick bent his head and ran his fingers through his hair. "I haven't talked to my mother in years. She walked out on me and my father when I was eight. She left me alone with him when he couldn't even take care of himself. I had to take care of him. And then when I couldn't take care of him anymore, they put him in the nuthouse."

Kelly felt a tear slide out of her eye and roll down her cheek. "You had to start taking care of your father when you were eight?"

Nick nodded.

"What happened after they put him in the hospital?" Kelly asked.

"I went to live with my aunt and uncle," Nick said.

"And your mother?"

Nick shrugged. "I don't know. After she left I hated her so much I never wanted to talk to her again."

"And you came here to find out what really happened," Kelly said. "Why wouldn't you tell me before?"

"If that was the story of *your* parents, would you go around telling everyone?"

"I guess not," Kelly admitted.

Nick came back to the bed and sat down beside her. "I really don't like it here any more than you do, Kelly. But somehow I feel I'm close to finding out what happened to my father. I can't explain it, but I feel like all these weird things that are happening are somehow related to what happened to him. I just want to stay here until I figure it out. And I'd really like it if you stayed too."

Kelly took his hand and squeezed it. "Okay. I'll stay here with you. But wouldn't it be easier if you just called your mother?"

"No!" Nick shook his head. "I hate her. I'll never talk to her again for as long as I live."

Chapter 23

The next morning as Kelly crossed the lobby on the way to the dining room, she noticed that there was no one at the front desk. In fact, the lights that usually lit the desk area were off.

In the dining room, the hot breakfast buffet had been set out, but there were no waiters or bus-boys clearing tables. Kelly got some toast and a cup of tea and sat down with the other lifeguards and Nick.

"Any word on Tiffany?" she asked.

"I spoke to the hospital earlier," Eric said. "She's definitely got a broken neck. They're still not sure whether she's going to be paralyzed."

The thought of Tiffany's horrible accident made Kelly feel sick. "I just don't get it," she said. "I've seen her do that dive a dozen times. She could do it in her sleep."

"Hey, don't forget," Eric said. "We're at the

143

New Arcadia. Headquarters of disaster."

"That reminds me," Kelly said. "Did anyone notice anything strange around here this morning?"

Eric and the others looked around. "Uh, no," Eric said.

"There's no one here," Kelly said. "The entire staff except for us is gone. The front desk was dark when I went past it."

"Maybe they're just getting a late start," Claire said.

"Somehow I don't think that's it," Kelly said.

"Well, who knows what the reason is," Nick said. "I mean, there could be a perfectly logical explanation. I really don't think we should let ourselves get carried away."

David, the new lifeguard, joined them. "Any word on Tiffany?" he asked.

David shook his head sadly as Claire filled him in on the news. "Listen," he said, "I know I'm new around here and everything, but this stuff is too weird for me. I mean, I've heard the stories about Chip and now Tiffany. I hate to say this, but I've pretty much decided I'm not going in that pool again."

"You mean you're quitting?" Kelly asked.

"Well, I wouldn't say that," David said. "I'll sit in the lifeguard chair. I'm just not going in the water unless it's a real emergency."

"Hey, listen, David," Eric said. "I've probably

been at this place longer than anyone. Now, I admit some weird stuff is happening, but I think your reaction is a little extreme."

"Maybe, but my job here is supposed to be making sure that the swimmers are safe," David said. "Risking my life wasn't part of the bargain."

"I think that's kind of chicken," Eric said.

"Well, I don't care what *you* think," David shot back.

"Wait a minute," Kelly interrupted them. "David's got a right to feel the way he does. Does anyone else feel that way?"

Claire looked around and then raised her hand. "I'm pretty nervous about going in the water too."

"Boy, you guys are really wimps," Eric said, shaking his head.

"Back off, Eric," Kelly warned.

"Well, I just don't see how anyone can be a lifeguard if they won't go in the water," Eric said.

"Well, we'll work it out," Kelly said. "There are only four of us left. We have to stick together."

After breakfast, the lifeguards were supposed to gather for their morning meeting. As Kelly walked down the hall to the pool, she had an eerie feeling. So far that morning, except for the lifeguards, she hadn't seen a single staff member—no housekeepers, no maintenance men, no bellboys. The guests at the inn just seemed to be going about their daily routines obliviously.

As Kelly entered the pool area, she noticed immediately that the pool water had become extremely cloudy—much worse than it had been the day before. She could barely see a foot beneath the surface.

"It's like soup," David said.

Kelly had to make a decision. The water wasn't just a little cloudy—it was like a dense fog.

"We're closing the pool," she said.

Nobody argued. They put signs on the doors saying the pool was closed until further notice.

"Does this mean we've got another day off?" Claire asked.

"I guess," Kelly said. David and Claire started to leave.

"Hey, wait, you guys," Eric said. "There's nothing to be scared of, and I'm going to prove it to you."

"What are you going to do?" Kelly asked.

"I'm gonna dive off the bad-luck diving board," Eric said. "Then I'm gonna swim to the bottom of the evil pool, and then I'm going to get out."

"There's no reason for you to do that," Kelly said.

"Yeah, there is," Eric said, staring at David.

As the others watched nervously, he climbed up onto the diving board and walked out to the end. "I'm afraid you may find this a bit of a disappointment compared to Tiffany," he said. "All I

146

know how to do is a regular old dive."

Eric sprang off the board and dove headfirst into the water. A second later he surfaced. "Ta da! As you can see, I dived off the board and lived to tell about it. Now I will swim to the bottom of the pool."

Kelly watched as Eric did a pike and went down. She knew she shouldn't worry, but just the same she did. The memory of Chip getting caught in the inrush of water around the drain came back to her, as did her own memory of something grabbing her ankle.

A moment later Eric surfaced in the middle of the pool. "Ta da, once again!" he said, treading water. "I know you couldn't see me, but you'll just have to take my word that I touched the bottom. Have I made my point? There's nothing to be scared of."

The words had hardly left his lips when his eyes suddenly went wide with alarm. "Hey! Ow!" he cried. "Ow! Ow! *OW!*"

"What is it?" Kelly gasped.

Eric began to thrash wildly toward the side of the pool. The water all around him was beginning to roil, and a pinkish foam was collecting on the surface.

"*Help!*" Eric screamed. "*Help! Ahhhhh!!!*"

Suddenly dozens of tiny fins began to cut through the water around him. Eric splashed and thrashed, but before anyone could do anything to help him, his eyes went blank, and his head disappeared under the boiling, foaming surface.

"Get the safety hook!" Kelly screamed.

David ran for the hook while the others watched in stunned silence. Then Eric's corpse floated briefly to the surface.

It was no longer recognizably a human body. Now it was just a reddish mass with gnawed, white bones sticking out of it. A second later it disappeared beneath the bloody surface again.

Claire hid her eyes and made choking sounds.

"Forget it," David said, dropping the hook on the ground. "It's too late."

"What . . ." Kelly gasped. "What the heck was that?"

"Piranhas," David said. Then he turned and walked quickly out of the pool area.

Chapter 24

Kelly sat on Nick's bed with her back against the wall. She was alone in his room, waiting. She still couldn't believe what she'd witnessed. The tiny fish had literally torn Eric to shreds. Kelly and Nick had locked the doors to the pool and come up to Nick's room because the lock on *his* door worked.

Now she sat there and waited while Nick went to get help.

Across the room, the doorknob turned.

"Who is it?" Kelly gasped. Everything frightened her now.

"It's me," Nick said, letting himself in and locking the door behind him.

"What happened?" Kelly asked quickly. "Did you tell anyone? Did you call the police?"

Nick nodded slowly. His expression said that the news wasn't good. "I called the police and told them that someone had been eaten by piranhas in the pool."

"They didn't believe you?" Kelly asked.

"Not only did they not believe me, but they tried to keep me on the line so they could trace the call," Nick said. "I told them I was calling from the New Arcadia Inn, but they didn't believe me. They were convinced that it was a crank call."

"What about telling someone around here?" Kelly asked.

Nick shook his head. "There's still no one at the front desk or in any of the offices. I heard some guests grumbling about the lousy service, and a few of them are even leaving. But most of the people just seem to be doing whatever they'd normally do on vacation—except swimming in the pool."

"You didn't see David or Claire, did you?" Kelly asked.

"Nope. I have a feeling they're both long gone, after what we saw this morning."

"I can't say I blame them," Kelly said with a shudder. She pulled her knees up to her chest and hugged them tightly. "To tell you the truth, I can't believe *we're* still here."

Nick came over and sat down on the bed beside her. "If you want, I can try to help you go. Maybe we can find someone who's leaving and arrange for you to get a ride with them."

Kelly looked up at him. "What about you?"

"I can't go," Nick said. "I'm certain that all this crazy stuff is somehow related to what happened to my father."

"But you have no proof," Kelly said.

"I know." Nick nodded. He looked sad and frustrated. Kelly slid close to him and put her arm across his shoulders.

"I wish I could get you to change your mind and leave with me," she whispered.

"You can't," Nick said. "I loved my father. Even when he was crazy and I had to take care of him, I knew that he was a good person. I knew something horrible and unfair had happened to him. When he died, I swore I'd find out what happened."

"But how?" Kelly asked. "What are you going to do now?"

Nick shrugged and hung his head. "I don't know." He looked up at Kelly. "I know this'll sound insane, but I feel as if all these accidents have been leading to something. Like it's all coming down to a final confrontation between me and whatever's out there." He looked in the direction of the spa. "Whatever's in the pool."

The thought frightened Kelly. She hugged him. "I hope not."

"Why?" Nick asked.

"Because I don't want anything to happen to you, Nick."

151

Nick turned his face toward her and their eyes met. Their lips moved slowly closer and closer until they touched. Kelly shut her eyes and clung to him. She'd never felt like she'd needed someone so badly in her life. Not just because of how much she liked him, but because he was her island of safety in the sea of swirling insanity that surrounded them.

"Can't you call her?" Kelly asked later, after they'd held each other and kissed for a long time.

"My mother?" Nick shook his head. "No. Never."

"But she might know," Kelly said. "She might be the only one who knows what happened to your father."

"I told you, I'll find out myself," Nick said.

"How?" Kelly asked. "Are you going to go down to the pool and try to talk to whatever's in it?"

Nick smirked.

"I'm not joking," Kelly said. "You've been through the files in the lifeguard office. You've probably looked in other places as well. Where are you going to turn next?"

Nick didn't answer. He just looked away.

"Do you know how to get in touch with her?" Kelly asked.

Nick stared at her. "Why is it so important to you?"

"It's important to me because it's important to you," Kelly said. "I can see how it's eating you up inside. If you can find an answer, I know I can get you to leave this place and never come back."

Nick sighed and shook his head. "I swore I'd never talk to her again, Kelly. You don't know what it did to my father when she left us. You don't know what it did to me."

"But by not calling her, you're just hurting yourself," Kelly said. "You're just making everything harder for yourself."

Nick looked away.

"Nick, just suppose you wanted to speak to her," Kelly said. "Do you know where she is? Do you know how to get in touch with her?"

"Yes."

"How?"

Nick looked at her with pleading eyes. "Kelly, I can't. You don't understand how much I hate her."

"I only asked if you knew how to get in touch with her," Kelly said.

"Well, every year my grandparents send me a Christmas card," Nick said. "I know they live in Sarasota, Florida. I guess I could call information and get their number. They should know where my mother is living now."

Nick didn't change his mind easily, but finally, after they talked about it for a long time, he did. They went down to the pay phone in the lobby and Nick dialed Florida information.

Suddenly Kelly realized that something was different. The inn wasn't nearly as crowded as it had been the day before, or even that morning. As she stood in the lobby, she watched a number of guests carry their bags out the front door. People were leaving.

"Okay, thanks," she heard Nick say as he hung up the phone. Kelly glanced at him, and he held up a pad with a phone number written on it. He'd gotten his mother's number.

But Nick didn't call her right away. He stood at the phone for a long time first. Finally he slipped some change into the coin slot and dialed the number. He waited, and then started to speak to someone.

"What? Oh, okay," Nick said. "I'll call back later."

"She wasn't home?" Kelly asked after he hung up.

"She won't be back until nine tonight," Nick said. "I'll have to call her then."

The day passed incredibly slowly. More and more guests were leaving, and the staff was nowhere to be seen. Nick and Kelly snuck into the kitchen and made themselves a meal. Later they walked past the indoor pool. The doors were closed and the signs were still up, saying the pool was closed.

The minutes crawled by until it was time to call again. They went back to the lobby. Nick dialed, and then turned to Kelly and nodded. She knew he must have reached his mother. Kelly stepped away from the phone booth to let Nick have some privacy.

Nick stayed on the phone for a long time. When he finally got off, he looked very somber. Kelly was dying to know if he'd found anything out. As Nick walked toward her, she couldn't hold her curiosity in any longer.

"Did she tell you?" she asked.

Nick nodded. "Yes, she told me."

Chapter 25

They went back to Nick's room. Kelly sat on the bed while Nick stood by the window.

"You won't believe this, but my father was a lifeguard here," he said.

"You're serious?" Kelly asked.

Nick nodded. "He worked here every summer, saving money for college. He met my mother here. She worked as a waitress and was saving to go to college too."

"None of the pictures show him in a lifeguard's uniform," Kelly said.

"My mother said he destroyed all those pictures," Nick said. "After it happened."

"What happened?"

Nick took a deep breath. "Here's the story. My mother and father were working here and saving for college. The problem was, they weren't saving nearly enough. At the rate they were going, they were never going to be able to afford tuition. That's just background that will make you understand what happened later."

Kelly nodded.

Nick continued: "My father had a friend named Jack. Jack was also a lifeguard, but he was different from my dad. He really didn't need the money; he was here to have a good time."

"Was he the one in the picture?" Kelly asked.

Nick nodded. "Jack's father was a big politician, and Jack's future was pretty much set from the day he was born. Anyway, Jack dated lots of girls. He was good-looking and wild, and girls liked him. Since he and my father were friends, they used to double-date a lot."

"And one of the girls he dated was the girl in the pictures?" Kelly guessed.

"Yes," Nick said. "She was sort of wild. One day she just showed up at the inn. No one knew where she came from. That might seem odd now, but back in the sixties things were looser. People floated around a lot more. Anyway, once Jack started dating this girl, she just wouldn't let go."

"A little like Tiffany and you until David showed up," Kelly said.

"From what my mother said, this girl was a lot worse," Nick said. "She started following Jack everywhere. She became a real pain. So one night Jack and this girl and my parents were up late, playing around at the pool. My mother got tired and went to bed, but the others stayed up. I guess maybe they were drinking a little. Anyway, something happened. The girl drowned."

Kelly stared at him with wide eyes. "Like the story we heard in the dining room."

"My father swore to my mother that it was an accident," Nick said. "The problem was, it still looked suspicious. Jack was convinced there would be an investigation, maybe even a trial. He was worried that it would not only ruin his career, but his father's career as well. So he told my father to go up to his room."

"I don't understand," Kelly said.

"The next day the girl was gone," Nick said. "Jack and my father never talked about what happened. But soon after that my mother and father both had enough money to go to college."

"So Jack told his father what had happened," Kelly guessed. "And his father gave your parents money for college to keep them quiet?"

Nick nodded and winced. Kelly guessed it must hurt him to think his father would do such a thing.

"So you think it was the guilt that made your father commit suicide?" Kelly asked.

Nick nodded. "And there's one other thing. The girl who died . . . her name was Laura."

"Like the bracelet we found near the building?" Kelly gasped.

Nick nodded.

"You don't think Jack really buried her out by the pool, do you?" Kelly asked.

"Why not?" Nick asked. "She disappeared that night. No one ever saw her again."

"But all we found was the bracelet," Kelly said. "The skeleton wasn't there."

"That's right," Nick said.

"You don't think . . ." Kelly began to say, then shook her head.

No, it was impossible.

"You felt it," Nick said. "It grabbed your ankle."

Kelly stared at him. "You can't be serious, Nick. This is crazy."

"There were *piranhas* in the pool this morning," Nick said. "That's not exactly normal, Kelly. Don't you see? Anything can happen here."

Kelly sat up. "Then I think we ought to leave right now, before something happens to us."

"I don't think you have to worry," Nick said.

"Why not?"

"Because it's the pool," Nick said. "That's where these things happen."

"But I first felt it grab me outside," Kelly said, "in the flooded ground near the filtration building."

"I know," Nick said. "But after that everything happened around the pool. I have a theory, Kelly, but it's going to sound totally nuts."

Kelly shrugged. "So what else is new?"

"I think that when the pipe broke, whatever it is that's doing all these things moved from the ground to the pool. It must be trapped there now."

Kelly shivered again and shook her head.

"You don't believe me?" Nick asked.

"I believe you, Nick. I just can't believe that I've gotten to the point where I do believe it."

Nick didn't answer. He had a distant look in his eye.

"What is it, Nick?" Kelly asked.

"I still don't get it," he said. "I mean, if it's really true that the drowning was an accident, why did it drive my father crazy?"

Kelly went over and put her arm around his shoulder. "You're going to drive *yourself* crazy trying to come up with answers, Nick. There's no way you can find out what really happened that night."

"I have to, Kelly. This thing's been bugging me my whole life. I have to know."

"Wait." Kelly had an idea. "You said Jack's father was a politician. Maybe you could find Jack. It's been a long time since Laura died. Maybe he'd tell you the truth."

Nick gave her a puzzled look. "Didn't I tell you about him before?"

"Tell me what?" Kelly asked.

"My mother said Jack died in a car accident. It was just a few weeks after the whole thing happened. He was driving to college for the first time."

"Then there's no way you'll ever know," Kelly said, disappointed.

Nick sat quietly for a long time.

"I still don't see why we shouldn't leave," Kelly said. "The staff is gone, the guests are leaving, the pool's closed. What's the point of staying?"

Nick nodded. "I guess you're right." He glanced out the window. "It's getting late. Let's leave in the morning."

Later, up in Nick's room, Kelly got into the bed while Nick lay down on the floor under a blanket. He turned the light off.

"You okay?" he asked in the dark.

"Yes," Kelly said. "Thanks. But I still feel bad about you sleeping on the floor."

"I don't mind."

Kelly lay awake in the dark, staring out the window at the stars. She doubted she'd be able to fall asleep soon.

"Kelly?"

"Yes?"

"You said you heard it laugh. You said it spoke to you."

"Yes," Kelly said. "Why?"

"No reason," Nick said. "I was just wondering. Well, good night."

Finally Kelly was able to drift off to sleep, dreaming of how things would all be okay in the morning. . . .

Chapter 26

It was still dark when Kelly opened her eyes. Bright moonlight shone in through the window. Kelly turned to look at Nick on the floor. But the blanket was thrown back and Nick was gone.

"Nick?" Kelly sat up in the dark. No one answered. She got out of bed and kneeled down to touch the blanket Nick had been sleeping under. The blanket felt warm. Nick must've just left.

The pool. Kelly felt a shiver run through her. Her stomach began to hurt. Now she knew why he'd asked her if it had spoken.

She got out of bed and went out into the hall, thankful that she had slept in her clothes. It was dark and very quiet. The hall lights were out. The inn felt deserted, but perhaps the remaining guests were simply asleep. Kelly walked quickly down to the elevator. She pushed the buttons, but they didn't light up. She pushed the buttons again.

Nothing happened. The elevator didn't make a sound.

Kelly ran to the stairway at the end of the hall. The red EXIT sign glowed. It seemed to be the only light in the inn that worked.

She ran down the stairs, crossed the dark lobby, and went down the long corridor that led to the indoor swimming pool. She reached the glass-enclosed pool and looked in. The lights were off, but in the moonlight she could see Nick's outline at the shallow end. He seemed to be kneeling near the edge of the pool.

Kelly reached for the door, but it was locked. She hurried along the windows until she was outside the shallow end.

"Nick!" she shouted and banged on the window, but he didn't seem to hear her. Kelly stared in. Nick was peering into the water. It looked as if he was talking to someone. Kelly stretched up on her toes, but she couldn't see if anything was there.

"Nick!" She banged against the window again. He had to hear her. Why didn't he turn around?

Suddenly she saw a ripple in the water in front of Nick. Inside, Nick stopped talking. Then he leaned closer to the edge of the pool and started talking again.

Kelly strained to see who he was talking to. But all she could see were ripples in the pool.

Suddenly something burst out of the water,

164

grabbed Nick, and yanked him back into the pool with a splash. Thrashing and fighting in the shallow end, Nick tried to stand up, but he was dragged under again and again. Kelly gasped and stared in frozen terror as Nick again struggled to the surface, this time dragging something up with him.

Kelly cried out in horror. The thing clinging to Nick was half human, half skeleton. One arm was bone from the elbow down. Its face was a skull, except for a few patches of flesh and long, stringy hair. But there was no doubt in Kelly's mind that it was the girl in the picture.

It was Laura.

"*Nick!*" Kelly screamed and banged on the windows. Laura was still trying to drown Nick. Nick fought and kicked at the monster. Kelly ran back to the doors and yanked on them as hard as she could, but they were locked tight.

There was nothing she could do except watch.

Down at the shallow end, Nick and Laura were locked in a deadly struggle. At one point, Nick hooked his arm around the silver rail of the pool ladder and began to pull Laura out. The decayed girl fought madly to pull Nick back into the pool. Its hideous mouth was agape and its one eye bulged. Nick managed to keep it out of the water for a long time. Kelly saw Laura's mouth open. It seemed as if the creature was having trouble breathing. Finally it got its skeleton hand around

Nick's throat and tore him away from the ladder.

They splashed back into the pool. Kelly gasped sharply, her hand frozen on the door handle. She had to get inside somehow to help him. Nick kicked and fought, but he seemed to be tiring. If Kelly didn't get there soon he'd surely die. She desperately looked around for a weapon, or something she could use to break the glass.

Then Laura crawled onto Nick's back and grabbed his head with her clawlike hand. No matter how hard he fought, Nick couldn't tear her off him.

Finally he tumbled forward with a splash and disappeared beneath the surface of the water.

It seemed as if a long time passed. Kelly pressed her face against the glass door and began to sob. "Oh, Nick, Nick . . ." she gasped as tears ran down her cheeks.

But he was gone.

Nick was dead.

Suddenly Kelly heard a laugh. Looking up, she saw Laura standing in the pool with her back to her.

Anger replaced Kelly's sorrow. She gritted her teeth and pushed hard against the glass door.

To her surprise, it opened easily.

Chapter 27

Kelly stepped inside and let the door close behind her.

"Ah ha ha haaaa!" Laura's laughter sent chills down Kelly's spine.

"Why did you kill him?" Kelly asked.

The laughter stopped. Laura turned in the water and stared at Kelly with the one eye in her half-skull face.

"He killed me," she said with a hideous smile.

It took Kelly a moment to understand. "No," she said. "His father might have killed you, but Nick didn't. He wasn't even born when you died."

"No matter," Laura said, wagging a skeleton finger at Kelly. "Come here, pretty girl."

Kelly walked toward the shallow end of the pool. "Are you certain his father killed you?"

"If not, they let me die," Laura said. "It makes no difference."

"But it could have been an accident," Kelly said.

"Yes, no, maybe." Laura was staring at Kelly's ankles. "I know you. You've gotten out of my grip twice. Come, let me try again."

Laura moved to the edge of the pool. Kelly trembled as she looked down and watched the monster reach for her ankle with her skeleton hand.

"Just come a little closer," Laura said, reaching out over the concrete that surrounded the pool.

Kelly gulped and moved a fraction of an inch closer. Meanwhile, Laura was stretching out of the pool toward her, her skeleton fingers only inches from Kelly's ankles.

"A little closer," Laura whispered with that hideous smile.

Kelly moved another fraction of an inch.

Suddenly Laura jumped halfway out of the pool and lunged for Kelly's ankle. But Kelly moved faster. She grabbed the skeleton hand at the wrist.

"What are you doing?" Laura screamed, pulling back and trying to yank her wrist out of Laura's grip.

But Kelly held tight. She and the creature were locked in a tug-of-war. Kelly wedged her feet against the base of the pool ladder and pulled with every ounce of strength she had. Very slowly, Laura slid farther out of the pool.

168

"*Noooooo!*" Laura screamed, grabbing the edge of the pool with her fleshy hand.

Kelly yanked as hard as she could, breaking Laura's grip on the pool's edge. A moment later she pulled Laura completely out of the water.

"I can't breathe," Laura gasped, writhing as Kelly dragged her away from the pool and out through the glass doors.

"I can't . . . I can't . . ." the creature gasped, still trying to twist her skeleton hand out of Kelly's grasp.

Kelly pulled her outside and across the grass. The sky was turning gray as dawn approached. By now Laura had ceased to gasp or talk. Finally Kelly let go. Laura lay still on the grass. Her hideous mouth was gaping open and her one eye stared blankly at the gray sky.

Kelly stood on the lawn of the New Arcadia for a long time, watching the thing that had once been Laura. But the creature was still, motionless, lifeless. The sky turned from gray to blue and pink in the east as the sun began to shine. Finally Kelly turned away and went back to her room, where she got her clothes and her CD player. The New Arcadia was empty and still. Kelly walked out the front doors and tried to remember the way back to the road and the bus stop.

She was going home.

≡ HarperPaperbacks *By Mail*

Read all of L. J. Smith's spine-tingling thrillers.

The Secret Circle

This new series from the bestselling author of The Vampire Diaries tells the thrilling story of Cassie, who makes a startling discovery when she moves to New Salem: She is the last of a long line of witches. Now she must seize her power or lose it forever. . . .

THE VAMPIRE DIARIES
by L.J. Smith

The romantic, terrifying chronicle of a dark love triangle: two vampire brothers and the beautiful girl who's torn between them.

Volume I: THE AWAKENING
Volume II: THE STRUGGLE
Volume III: THE FURY
Volume IV: THE REUNION

Look for:
TEEN IDOL
by Kate Daniel

Volume I: THE INITIATION
Volume II: THE CAPTIVE
Volume III: THE POWER